TH

H

NATALIE FOX

MILLS & BOON

MILLS & BOON LIMITED
ETON HOUSE, 18-24 PARADISE ROAD
RICHMOND, SURREY TW9 1SR

13A

*First published in Great Britain 1995
by Mills & Boon Limited*

© Natalie Fox 1995

*Australian copyright 1995   Philippine copyright 1995
This edition 1995*

ISBN 0 263 78930 6

*Set in Times Roman 10½ on 12 pt.
01-9504-50800 C*

Made and printed in Great Britain

CHAPTER ONE

'ARE you absolutely sure that is Hugo Drake-Latimer?' Angel asked the receptionist, nodding in the direction of the couple dining in the small, intimate restaurant across the hall of the hotel. Surely she had misheard the head waiter as he had led him and his lovely companion to their table, and surely she had misheard the owner of the hotel earlier when he had mentioned he would be dining here tonight?

Angel almost willed the receptionist to deny it because this chance sighting of the man who had ruined her cousin's life was spooky. She had only been talking about Claudia's disastrous affair this very morning.

'Think yourself lucky, Angel, darling,' Patrick had told her with self-satisfaction as she had driven him to the ferry that morning. 'There are no waves in our life and I don't intend there to be in the future. Life is what you make it——'

'Shut up, Patrick,' Angel had murmured as she'd come to a smooth halt behind a container lorry at the traffic-lights. She'd had all she could take of Patrick's holier-than-thou attitude to love and passion, and Angel had wished she'd never told him about Claudia's affair and its horrendous consequences. She might have known he wouldn't understand, but there again, she wasn't so sure she understood herself.

5

Poor Claudia, so obsessed by that man and then to be so cruelly cheated and rejected by him. It had hit her badly and she'd declined into a crushing depression that no amount of support from the family could drag her out of. Angel could well understand her feeling angry and cheated over the loss of a great deal of money to the man, but to love him still? It must have been some love, a passion that Angel had never experienced and couldn't really understand. But then Claudia was a passionate and dramatic type whereas Angel wasn't. Her life was quite simple and secure.

Hugo Drake-Latimer's dining companion this night was beautiful and was very probably one of many, Angel surmised. So not only was he a con man of the very lowest order but a wretched womaniser as well. Poor Claudia.

'Yes, I'm sure it's Mr Drake-Latimer,' the receptionist told Angel in a secretive whisper. 'He always dines here when he comes to the Lakes.' She made it sound as if it was a privilege to have him here. 'Are you dining in tonight, Miss Weston?'

Angel *hadn't* planned to dine in tonight; in fact she hadn't even planned on booking into this hotel at all after dropping Patrick at the ferry. Patrick hated flying. He had business in Dublin and Angel had a week's spring leave on her hands. She still wasn't quite sure how it had happened, this sudden need inside to do something different. She suspected it might be something to do with Patrick's remark about no waves in his life. She was a part of his life so therefore no waves for her either, and that thought niggled a bit.

So she had let this impulse for change take her over. Like some quirky little will-o'-the-wisp it had crept into her psyche and shaken the bones of her regular life.

She had driven home to Manchester where she shared a house with Claudia, found the place bleak and desolate without her normally fiery cousin, who had been whisked away for a Corfu break by her concerned father, packed a few things together and headed north to the Lake District. An impulse, a whim? She'd never suffered from them before. Her life was orderly and safe...

'Yes, yes, I think I will,' Angel responded with a warm smile. 'And do you think I could have the table by the ingle-nook? The log fire looks so tempting.'

And the position would give her clear sight of Hugo Drake-Latimer, because suddenly she was overwhelmed by yet another odd impulse. She was immensely curious to find out what made a man like him, who to outward appearances looked as if he was capable of running his life legitimately, swindle and seduce beautiful women and disappear out of their lives without a backward glance of regret. And wasn't she also perhaps secretly nurturing a fantasy of exposing this man?

Yes, she could see it all. Angel Weston bringing this man to justice, laying bare his little schemes, gaining moral revenge for her cousin, not to say anything of recovering the tens of thousands of pounds— Claudia's divorce settlement after a disastrous marriage—that she'd invested with this man, only to lose it all on a massive share plunge, or so he had said.

Once in her bedroom Angel stared at herself in disbelief in the dressing-table mirror. What on earth was happening to her? Here she was, miles from the security of her home and her job, staying in a strange hotel and plotting the downfall of a man who had certainly done her no harm. Oh, but he had nearly destroyed Claudia. Her cousin had loved the man, trusted him enough to hand over her money and her heart, and now look at the state of her. All her confidence gone, depressed and inconsolable, it would take her years to rebuild her life.

Angel brushed out her dark brown hair and flicked it around her shoulders, and wondered at her sudden nerve. Normally she wore her hair up on the top of her head—Patrick preferred it that way. Normally she didn't wear so much mascara or eye-shadow—Patrick didn't like it. Normally she wouldn't wear this figure-hugging black dress, an impulse buy on the way to the Lakes. Patrick would have a fit...

And Patrick isn't here, Angel mused to herself as she went down to the restaurant. Maybe this was what all this was about, she thought as the waiter showed her to the table by the ingle-nook. Rebellion. She felt sure a marriage proposal from Patrick was imminent and...and she didn't know. She loved him, yes, she did, but...

She caught Hugo Drake-Latimer's eye almost immediately she sat down as the waiter fussed her into her seat.

He had dark eyes and they were penetrating, treacherous and very sexy eyes. Angel felt herself go hot all over and doubted it was the proximity of the logs blazing in the grate a few feet from her. Hugo Drake-Latimer had that effect on her, and obviously on the woman he was dining with, who was gazing dreamily at him, and Claudia and all the other women he had conned. He was a charmer, no doubt of that. Beautifully strong-featured, with those unsubtle brows arched over those damned sexy dark eyes, a perfectly straight nose, clearly defined lips and a glimpse of exceptionally white teeth which she felt sure, if she stared hard enough, would give off a dazzling twinkle like a cartoon character.

And his hair was dark, with flashes of silver where silver should not be on a man who couldn't be older than thirty-four or -five. He was broad-shouldered and though he was sitting down she knew he was tall. A dinner-jacket would be out of place in this quaint old beamed family-run hotel, but the dark navy lounge suit he wore wouldn't be out of place at the Ritz. A crisp white shirt and a daring multicoloured silk tie at his throat said quite a lot. Conservative and trustworthy when needed, and a bit of a rogue at heart. A lot of a rogue at heart, Angel mentally corrected. Damn him! *All* rogue at heart.

Angel quietly ordered something simple, noticing that the con man and the woman who was probably his next victim were a course ahead of her, so if she skipped an appetiser she might end up level-pegging with them.

He'd lost interest in her, Angel noticed with relief, and as she sipped her mineral water her acute hearing tuned into the glamorous couple's conversation at the table across from her.

'That's my advice, Caroline. Take it or leave it. On your head be it if you don't, but I promise you you'll be wise to take heed of what I say.'

His voice was low and seductive and Angel could see Caroline already mentally signing on the dotted line.

'Yes, of course, Hugo. I'm listening to what you say and I know it would be sensible, but give me time to mull it over in my mind. I'm not ready to make a decision yet.'

Oh, God, Angel thought in misery. He was doing it again, setting up another victim. Poor Caroline, but at least the lovely lady was exercising a measure of caution. However, the night was young! Angel stared at her lemon sole as if it had two heads. What should she do? Warn Caroline? Heavens, she looked very capable of looking after herself, but then Claudia had appeared that way too and look what had happened to her.

There was laughter, and the gorgeous strawberry-blonde leaned towards the dastardly Hugo and kissed him lightly on the cheek. Whatever she murmured to him was lost on Angel—something intimate, no doubt, otherwise why lower the voice? Angel looked up and was shocked to see those sexy dark eyes directed her way again. The nerve of him!

Coffee was served, by which time Angel was feeling extremely uncomfortable. The con man's eyes had scarcely left her—not that Angel had been gawping at him to know, but she just instinctively felt that he had been watching her most of the course of the meal. It had sent prickles of awareness down her spine, but she had no fear that her features might jog his memory because she resembled her cousin little. Claudia was much darker and more sultry, sort of exotic-looking, whereas Angel was...well, ordinary-looking, she supposed. 'Interesting-looking', Patrick had described her. 'Not beautiful,' he'd teased, 'but certainly worth a second look...'

They were leaving, Hugo and Caroline. But where were they going? They weren't staying here. At least, Hugo Drake-Latimer wasn't. Earlier Angel had been enquiring about local tours at Reception and had overheard the owner of the hotel telling the head waiter that he was expected for dinner tonight. Angel's heart had leapt wildly in her ribcage because there couldn't possibly be two people in the world by the name of Hugo Drake-Latimer!

The name had thrummed through her with disbelief. Claudia's lover, Claudia's deceiver, coming to this very hotel this evening! It was impossible, unbelievable, and Angel had wondered if some divine interceptor had guided her here to take revenge on her cousin's lover...

Drake-Latimer was helping Caroline on with her wrap. They were both leaving! Where were they going, his home or hers? Suddenly Angel knew what she must do...

'Mother of God, I must be out of my mind!' Angel hissed to herself. She shivered and huddled into her Aran cardigan, the one she always left in the car in case of emergencies. She had flown out of the hotel after them, not having time to leap up to her room for more suitable clothing. It was spring, but the Lake District was anything but warm and spring-like. The daffodils and tulips might be in bloom but no one had told the weather. Rain and lake mists were in abundance.

Angel hadn't minded earlier when she had trudged through the pine forests around the lake in her oiled jacket and boots. Somehow the weather had suited her pensive mood then, but now she wasn't pensive. She felt as if an electrical charge was running through her, out of control and... and yes, it was very exciting. She was *casing a joint*. Angel Weston had actually had the nerve to follow the man and his companion out of the hotel and, keeping a discreet distance from the Mercedes in front, had trailed them here to a very elegant town house in the main street of a quiet village.

Hugo Drake-Latimer had left his car lights on, so she surmised that this was Caroline's home and he would be out shortly. She felt like a private detective, and wondered if her true vocation lay in that line instead of working her socks off as personal secretary to the managing director of a chain of hotels.

Heart on hold, Angel watched as Hugo emerged from the house and ran lightly down the steps to his car. Yes, he had a definite spring of anticipation in his step. Was his latest scam working? Angel waited till he'd drawn away from the kerb and rounded a corner and then she was in hot pursuit.

Ten minutes later Angel splashed to a wet halt and peered in disbelief through the windscreen. It seemed as if the Mercedes had just disappeared into a lake.

She could see the silvery water shimmering menacingly in the distance; the Mercedes had been heading that way and then—disappeared.

Suddenly she saw the tail-lights and realised he was crossing a causeway to the other side. Once the lights had faded Angel shifted the gear into first and edged forward. Her Escort seemed to be sucked into a fine mist and it was a struggle to see clearly, then suddenly the mist swirled away and she drove steadily across the causeway thinking that if she didn't keep a perfectly straight course she'd be up to the wheel axles in lake water.

It was then that Angel began to panic and see the folly of her ways. This was ridiculous. She was up against a wall of mist and no road to speak of, no Catseyes to guide her. She didn't even know if she was across the lake or not. She slowed, and then to her horror realised she was face to face with a stone wall. Slamming the brakes on, she skidded to a halt, stalled the engine, and almost immediately the car door was wrenched open and Angel screamed as hard as she could.

'And cut that out!' was the sharp order as a hand shot inside the car and released her seatbelt. She was hauled unceremoniously and unfettered out of the driver's seat to face the fury of Hugo Drake-Latimer in the pouring rain.

'What the hell do you think you're doing?' Angel cried, trying to fidget her way out of his grasp but failing dismally because he was so strong. Her car lights still blazed and she could see him, but little else, in the unnerving gloom. Her feet skidded in mud and shingle and she thought her last moment had come prematurely.

He released her and she fell back against her car, her hands going protectively to her throat.

'Well, I'm not going to throttle you,' he mocked and then added lethally, 'Yet. What's the idea, following me here? Who are you and what do you want?'

The questions came like machine-gun fire and Angel was quick to return the blast. 'I'm lost,' she blurted, her brain working overtime. He might believe her— he *must*! 'It's so misty and I'm a stranger to these parts and—— What on earth are you doing?'

Once again his hand had shot inside her car, this time to extinguish her car lights and remove the ignition key. He slammed the door shut and, taking her arm, tried to frogmarch her to...where? She couldn't see a thing!

'Where are you taking me? If you start anything I'll fight you,' she spat venomously. 'I've done self-defence...I can bring you down with one lethal blow——'

'Spare me,' he growled in an I-don't-believe-a-word-of-it tone.

She was propelled forward ahead of him and suddenly she saw a house in front of her. A grey stone cottage with variegated ivy clinging around the porch. A wooden tub of pink azaleas stood to one side of the white front door, a stately potted bay tree to the other side, all suddenly illuminated by a beam of light from a torch he had just switched on. He pushed open the door and urged Angel inside, but she swung on him as soon as she was over the threshold.

'How dare you do this to me?' she blazed. Remarkably she wasn't afraid and she supposed it was because of what she knew about him from Claudia. Womanising con men didn't rape or murder or kidnap—they just used their charms to get what they wanted. Hearts and money.

'And how dare you follow me?' he retaliated brusquely, his dark brows drawn together in anger. 'You watched me through dinner all evening at the hotel and now you've hounded me to my home, and I take great exception to my privacy being invaded.'

'Privacy!' Angel stormed, pushing her tousled brown hair off her brow. 'I didn't force my way into this house; you dragged me in. I was lost and——'

'You were lost on my private property——'

'Don't be ridiculous. I was crossing the lake, not following you, I assure you. I must have taken a wrong turning and——'

'And there isn't a wrong turning to take,' he interjected.

'Well, I did!' Angel insisted and then calmed herself. Shouting at him wasn't going to get her anywhere. 'Now, if you accept my apology, I'll be on my way.'

She went towards the door but he kicked it shut with a backward swipe of his foot. He didn't take his eyes from her.

'Too late, I'm afraid,' he told her levelly.

'It's never too late,' Angel retorted. 'Think about that before I start screaming my head off.'

He looked amused and shook his head. 'Now, why in heaven's name should you scream your head off? I certainly won't give you cause to.'

'You already have. You have dragged me into your lair and ... and ...'

He smiled then and leaned back against the door, folding his arms across his chest. 'And? Go on. I'll be interested to hear what your imagination has come up with to explain my actions.'

Angel didn't know what to say. Her eyes suddenly took in her surroundings. They were standing in a fair-sized hallway with a dog-leg staircase rising up to the next floor. There was thick, warm carpet beneath her feet and original landscapes on the walls and mellowed mahogany furniture. The overall feeling was one of security and she wasn't afraid, and yet ...

Angel found her voice at last. 'You'd better let me go because I'm staying at the White Swan hotel and they will raise the alarm if I don't return soon.'

He unfolded his arms, reached across to the hall table and picked up a mobile phone. He held it out to her. 'Call them. Tell them where you are——'

'I don't know where I am!' Angel retorted triumphantly. 'I'm lost, remember?'

'You're at Greystone Cottage——'

'A prisoner!'

He looked at her with the contempt he might hold for a belligerent schoolgirl.

'A prisoner you are not, an overnight guest you definitely are,' he told her firmly.

'An overnight guest?' Angel exploded, alarm raising her voice. Surely he didn't intend to force her to stay with him all night?

'Sadly, yes,' he drawled as he put the phone down on the table. 'I don't want it and you obviously find the idea abhorrent, but really there is no alternative but for you to stay the night here.'

'There is a very sane alternative,' she told him, lifting her chin. 'You give me back my ignition keys, which I notice you confiscated into your pocket, and you open that door and you let me leave. I'll go back the way I came and——'

'And end up in the lake,' he told her, not without a certain satisfactory hum to his tone.

'I didn't end up in the lake getting here!'

'But you will trying to get out of here.'

'I will not!' she protested. 'Not if you give me directions.'

'Wish that I could,' he said wearily, and leaned back against the door again. 'Have you any idea where you are?'

Actually Angel had absolutely no idea how far she had come tonight, what direction she had taken and if she would ever get back to the hotel in one piece. She'd been concentrating so hard on not losing sight of the Mercedes in front of her that she had taken little notice of her surroundings.

'No... not really,' she murmured. 'Across the lake somewhere.'

He smiled again and shook his head again, and when he did that he made her feel very small and stupid—*again*.

'Which lake?'

Angel shrugged and said rather idiotically, 'Seen one lake, you've seen them all.'

'You haven't a clue where you are, have you?'

She lowered her head and shook it slightly, very subdued now. 'None at all,' she admitted.

She heard him give out a weary sigh—or was it a bored one? Yes, very probably bored, she decided.

'You were so determined to follow me tonight, you put yourself at risk by not even noting where you were going.'

She lifted her head and looked at him warily. The man wasn't a fool but he obviously thought her one. She couldn't think of one good excuse to come up with to explain her strange behaviour tonight, not to him or herself. However had she allowed herself to get into such a situation? On that inward query she thought of Patrick. He wouldn't believe she was capable of such a thing, driving up to the Lake District on impulse, surveying this man over dinner on impulse, following this man to his home on impulse. He wouldn't believe it, absolutely not.

'I wasn't following you,' she lied in a small voice. Lies didn't come easily to her but this was certainly an essential exception. The man was a crook and if he thought she knew . . . She couldn't imagine how he would react but certainly not with pleasure. 'I . . . I don't know how I got here. I . . . I was restless after my meal and thought I'd go for a drive.'

His eyebrows came up in an expression of doubt, but he didn't say a word.

'I... I just drove and if I ended up here it was pure coincidence. Honestly!' She was getting used to this lying and getting quite good at it because he wasn't looking so doubtful now. 'So... so I'll leave now and I'm sure once I hit the main road I'll know exactly where I am. I'm... I'm sorry for invading your privacy and I'm sorry you thought...'

She didn't finish for he had leaned towards the front door and flicked a switch. Putting the outside lights on for her? That was promising. Then he looked at her and nodded towards the stairs, and when she stared at him blankly he indicated with a thrust of his thumb that she should go up.

'Just a minute...' she started to protest, a flush of wild colour rising up from her neck. Her clenched palms suddenly felt hot and sticky.

'No evil intentions, I assure you,' he said wearily, and somehow that stabbed at Angel.

She was hardly his type. His types were luscious rich women like Claudia and that Caroline, not second-lookers such as herself.

'So... so why?' she managed to breathe, her dark eyes wide with curiosity.

'To show you something you don't know.' He brushed past her and led the way but Angel didn't follow; she couldn't. Her feet felt like lead blocks. He turned at the bottom step.

'Look, sweetheart, I like my women with more flesh, more brains and a better sense of direction than you have, so you can let that fluttering heart of yours relax. I'm not going to touch you——'

'You arrogant bastard!' she exclaimed. That was one for Claudia.

He raised a very surprised brow at her outburst, and surely there was a glimmer of humour in those dancing grey eyes of his?

'Keep that up, lovely, and I might be reassessing you and finding something I like. Now follow me and listen and learn, and then you'll understand what I've been driving at.'

He proceeded up the stairs, quite confident that she would follow. Angel hesitated. She could make a bolt for the door but there would be little point in that because he had her car keys. She could run to the nearest house, though. It wasn't too late; someone might be up and able to help her.

'Are you coming of your own free will or shall I come down and——?'

'I'm coming,' Angel cried churlishly, and stepped towards the stairs. She was mad, quite out of her brains. Patrick would have her certified for this, following a strange man upstairs, a man who had taken her car keys, dragged her into his house and . . . and made it quite plain she wasn't his type.

He was standing by the landing window when she got to the top of the stairs.

'Come here,' he said quietly.

She went and stood by his side, careful not to get too close.

'What do you see?'

Angel gazed out of the window. The switch he had flicked by the door had indeed been the outside lights.

Everything was illuminated clearly and the mist wasn't so dense now.

She quelled an impatient sigh. This was silly; he was treating her like a child.

'What do you see?' he repeated.

'What is this, I spy with my little eye?'

'Get on with it,' he grated impatiently.

'My car, your car in the garage with the doors open, a brick wall, a garden gate, cuddly toy, set of glasses with decanter——' She didn't finish her sarcastic scrolling.

'Beyond the garden,' he snapped.

Angel strained her eyes. 'Water.' She shrugged. Water? her brain registered. Where was the causeway, the road across the lake they had both driven on to get here?

He grasped her arm and half pushed her into another room and across it to the window.

'And what do you see from this window?'

The back of the house was illuminated as well and Angel gazed out over a wide expanse of lawn sprinkled with daffodils and grape hyacinths sloping down to... water and more water.

He took her to the next room and another and the view was much the same from all four corners of Greystone Cottage—water.

'I...I don't understand,' she murmured as she stared out over the water. The moon had broken through and mist swirled in patches over the gunmetal sheet of uncompromising water. They were surrounded by it.

Angel felt as if she was in a dream-like state—disorientated and heady. She felt his closeness at her side as he held back the drapes for her to look out of the window. She smelt his warmth and the faintest of tantalising colognes. The swirling mist outside had seeped into her brain—it felt fuzzy with this muggy awareness of his presence. In horror she turned to face him in the darkness, and the lights outside were sufficiently bright to illuminate his features.

'We're on an island,' he told her, his voice suddenly soft, as if he was breaking bad news to her. 'My island, Summer Island. It's a very small island. This house is the only one on it. I like my privacy and I don't have a boat. Do you understand now?'

Angel stared at him with brown eyes as wide as saucers. Oh, yes, she understood all right. She was marooned here with him. That was what he had been trying to tell her but she hadn't listened. She was marooned in this cosy little cottage on this cosy little island with a man who was far from cosy. He was a con man, a womaniser, a charmer... And she had nothing to fear, she thought determinedly. Absolutely nothing, because she had absolutely nothing that could possibly interest him. Her heart was well protected by Patrick, her bank account was virtually nonexistent and he had already told her what sort of women he preferred. She didn't fit his bill in any shape or form.

'Yes . . . yes, I understand,' she murmured, and her voice only cracked very slightly.

CHAPTER TWO

'You don't sound very sure of that,' Hugo Drake-Latimer said quietly.

Angel stepped back from him and looked quickly round the room. Though there was no light she could see enough to know it was a bedroom. It seemed she might occupy it tonight. She suppressed a shiver of fearful anticipation at the thought. Strange man, strange surroundings. She'd never sleep a wink.

'I understand that we are surrounded by water but what I don't understand is how. I drove on concrete, on a road, a causeway.'

'And the rising water has cut us off,' he told her, letting the drapes at the window drop back into place.

'A tide! You don't have tides on a lake.'

'I didn't mention a tide,' he told her. 'I said rising water. This small lake is fed by waterfalls and a network of streams and when it rains——'

'The water rises,' Angel finished for him. 'And if the rain doesn't stop?'

He smiled. 'It usually does, eventually.'

'Eventually?' Angel breathed quietly. 'Supposing it doesn't? I mean, supposing it rains for days and weeks or months and the water gets higher and higher? The house could be flooded, washed away.'

He shrugged as if it really wasn't a problem or something he wanted to deal with at this precise moment. He moved to the door. 'The cottage is built on high ground and flooding hasn't happened before, and I don't waste time on wondering what would happen if it did. Life is far too short for hysterical predictions.'

A man who didn't want to face the real world? Angel wondered as she followed him downstairs. Yes, she supposed he lived in an odd, unreal vacuum, cheating women and playing with their emotions. She wondered if he ever felt any remorse for what he did to his victims.

'Don't you think it a bit short-sighted of you not to have a boat? It seems this area has the highest rainfall in the galaxy. A boat would surely be a wise investment.'

'I'm not a boating person,' he told her as he opened the door of a large sitting-room and switched on several table-lamps.

The first sight that hit Angel was the grand piano in one corner. It was magnificent, a satinwood beauty. Its presence surprised her. She wondered if it was for show or use.

'So . . . so what happens now?' she asked in a small voice. 'I mean, I understand now that . . . well . . . I must stay here.' Another thought struck her. How long before the water subsided?

'Yes, that is a certainty, though you could sleep in your car.' His eyes locked with hers, almost daring her to consider it.

'Whatever you think, I'm not short on brain power,' she told him. 'I'd be stupid to want to sleep in my car when you've offered me the comfort of your home for the night.' How brave and in control she was sounding.

One very dark brow rose teasingly. 'It could be more than one night. It could be three or seven or twelve.'

Angel forced a weak smile. 'I'm not easily frightened so you needn't bother trying to raise my blood-pressure.'

'Hmm.' His eyes raked her up and down and Angel felt the heat. 'Fear isn't the only way to raise the blood-pressure,' he said coolly.

He was in control, but Angel felt her own slipping sideways. That was a very suggestive thing to say and she saw what women saw in him. He was a very dangerous charmer but she had the advantage of hindsight via Claudia to guide her. He didn't know it but she knew all about him and forewarned was forearmed.

'That *double entendre* doesn't frighten me either,' she told him stoically.

He smiled silkily and stepped towards her. Angel's stomach knotted. He stood before her, tipped her chin and gazed down into her dark eyes. 'I wasn't referring to *your* blood-pressure, lovely,' he said softly.

In spite of her protestations she felt hers rise. Now she was scared—not terrified but certainly on her toes. But he was a teaser as well as a charmer, she told herself in an effort to control the situation.

'You have nothing to fear from me,' she murmured.

'Haven't I?' He slid his thumb over her chin and then lowered his hand, but didn't move away from her. 'If you want the truth *you* worry *me*,' he added mysteriously.

Angel raised her brows. 'Why should I worry you?' she asked innocently. She couldn't think what he was getting at. Then she felt heat course through her again. Surely he didn't think she was out to seduce *him*?

'I have every reason to feel I'm on thin ice here. You studied me intently all through dinner, followed me to my summer retreat, stalled your car in my own yard and here you are in my home for the night or more. I'm no hero, Miss whatever-your-name-is, and I certainly won't be turning my back on you and I'll certainly be locking my bedroom door tonight.'

Angel opened and shut her mouth like an oxygen-starved guppy, and then her voice came in bubbling tumult.

'I'm not here to seduce you,' she blurted indignantly.

'Oh, I know that, sweetheart,' he drawled. 'If you were you'd have shot up those stairs after me a darned sight quicker than you did.' He looked at her critically. 'The thought of being seduced by a beautiful woman doesn't hold fear for me, but how do I know you're not a troubled lady, jilted by your lover and wanting revenge on mankind in general?'

Her eyes widened enormously. 'Don't be ridiculous!' Angel cried, half laughing, half taking him seriously.

'Am I being ridiculous? I think not. Someone could make a pretty scary film out of this evening. Beautiful woman alone in isolated hotel set amid swirling misty lakes, eyeing the man dining across from her and envying the woman he is dining with. Following them out into the dank, wet night, rising water stranding them on his island. No way out or in. Silver blades flashing in the dead of night——'

'Stop it!' Angel cried again, still not sure if he was teasing her or not. But he must be. He couldn't be serious. 'I've not been rejected, I don't envy your girlfriend and I couldn't harm a mouse if my life depended on it!'

He smiled again and Angel could have sworn those glamorous teeth sparkled. He *was* teasing her, having fun at her expense.

'I know,' he said softly to placate her. 'But you get my point, don't you? These days a man can be as uncertain of a woman's motivations as a woman can be of a man's.'

So he was as wary of her as she was of him. Angel thought *she* was treading thin ice here but it didn't stop her retorting, 'If you feel threatened and vulnerable it suggests you have something to feel threatened and vulnerable about.'

He looked blankly at her, as if he didn't know what she was getting at, and now that she had said it she hoped he didn't understand. If he suspected she knew anything about him it could be very tricky indeed.

'I'm not sure I get the point of that,' he returned, and gave a small, dismissive shrug of his not so small and dismissive shoulders. 'And I'm too tired to struggle with it. Would you like a coffee or something stronger maybe—brandy or whisky—or are you a cocoa person last thing at night?'

He was something else, this Hugo Drake-Latimer.

'Look, all this is impossible,' she started. 'I can't stay here.'

'You haven't a choice; you really haven't.'

'But I have no clothes, no toothbrush.'

'Not really a problem set against the hazard of trying to swim across the lake.'

'I wasn't thinking of that——'

'I don't think you've been thinking at all this evening.'

That was true. Look where her impulses had led her so far. She hoped she had no more tonight because she could end up going the same way as Claudia. She watched him thoughtfully as he slid out of his suit jacket and bent down to light the fire. Logs were piled on a mound of kindling and screwed-up newspaper in the grate, and she watched him and the blue flames licking the wood, her eyes flashing from one to the other in rapid succession. To be truthful, she could understand Claudia's falling for him. He had it all—a glib tongue, good looks, and he was probably worth a few bob, albeit ill-gotten gains. He had this lovely cottage too, and she bet he didn't bring his women here. It was a retreat, somewhere he came when things got a bit hot for him in the real world.

Knowing what she knew, why wasn't she afraid? Twice he had indicated that she was beautiful—yes, she had counted. No one else had ever said she was beautiful—or was it just a figure of speech he used on all his women to flatter them into parting with their money and their hearts? Whatever, it hadn't unnerved her too much. Maybe it was because she was so down-to-earth and not living in outer space most of the time like Claudia.

'What's it to be, then?' He stood up from the fire and faced her.

'I beg your pardon?'

'Coffee, tea, cocoa, hydrochloric acid?'

'You're weird,' she murmured. 'Some imagination you have. What do you do in your spare time, plot horror movies?'

He smiled. 'No, but I write crime novels in my spare time.'

Angel couldn't help taking a sharp breath. Claudia had never mentioned that.

'Do you really?' she breathed. Was this another wind-up?

'Yes, really. Now, as you can't make a decision for yourself, can I make one for you? You go upstairs and switch on the electric blanket in the back bedroom—the bed will need the chill taken off it. Freshen up if you wish—I'm afraid we'll have to share the only bathroom—and then come down and we'll introduce ourselves to each other.'

She stared at him blankly. She couldn't stay; she just couldn't.

He read her thoughts and shrugged in resignation. 'No choice, sweetheart. I'm the only refuge. You stay here in warmth and comfort or you brave the lake, breast-stroke.'

'No choice,' she muttered despondently, and turned away. He followed her out into the hallway and as she took the first step on the staircase he went into the kitchen without a glance at her. Slowly Angel went upstairs, wondering if this was all a dream.

The back bedroom. She stepped into it and switched on the light. It was a large room with a huge double bed and the furnishings were bright chintz. She wondered who out of his girlfriends furnished this room, because men never went for chintz. Patrick loathed it.

Angel sat on the edge of her bed, grabbed a lacy cushion and hugged it to her chest. What on earth was she doing here? She felt almost tearful with the shock of it all. She wasn't going to cry, though, because her mascara wasn't waterproof and she had no cleanser with her... Hell, she had nothing with her!

Flinging the cushion down, she went to find the bathroom. It was pleasant enough, more masculine, with a white suite with gold taps and dark wood shelves and fitments. She opened the cabinet on the off chance that he had a new toothbrush lying around. There were several, and she unwrapped one and used it. Then she used his soap and his towel and thought how strange all this was.

Claudia should see her now. In that man's bathroom, making herself at home. No one would believe her.

She went back to the bedroom, groped by the side of the bed for the electric blanket switch and switched it on, then she went to stand by the window and reflect on all Claudia had told her about the man. He worked in investments and they had met in a hotel bar in Manchester and their affair had accelerated with the speed of Concorde. 'Love at first sight', Claudia had wailed in one of her worst moments. He'd wined and dined her in small, intimate restaurants on the outskirts of Manchester and they had danced in out-of-town night-spots and once he had whisked her away to Paris for the weekend, and then soon after had come the crunch. No more phone calls and, remarkably, she had no way of contacting him. On hearing that Angel had thought he must be married, but she hadn't mentioned her suspicions to her cousin because Claudia was upset enough already. And then there had been contact—one last phone call to tell her her investment had collapsed and he would be in touch again, but he never had been.

'Creep!' Angel cursed under her breath. She must keep reminding herself what a rat he was because if she ever forgot... How could she forget? But he was a charmer and Claudia's deep depression was all due to him, as if she hadn't suffered enough over the breakdown of her marriage. He'd swept her off her feet at a particularly vulnerable time of her life. She had fallen in love with the man—'true love', she had stated miserably, and Angel had believed her. And strangely, for all the wrong reasons, she envied her cousin that love even though it had been thrown back in her face so cruelly.

Angel had never felt so intensely passionate about Patrick. Their love had sprung from a long friendship formed through work contact. Patrick was in computers and they had met when he had been contracted to set up new systems in the group of hotels she worked for, the latest being the luxurious riverside hotel, which was officially opening in a couple of week's time. Patrick had been more than pleased to get that contract and it had fuelled the thought that a marriage proposal was in sight. Patrick wouldn't risk marriage until he was absolutely secure in the knowledge that he could provide for a wife. That was his way.

Yes, she was comfortable with him, safe and secure, and that was how love was for her. She couldn't be like Claudia, hysterical and highly charged by passion, because it just wasn't in her make-up, and yet . . . and yet there was still a feeling that she might be missing out on something. But it was only a vague feeling, something that assailed her occasionally when she was overworked and overtired. It didn't mean anything.

With a sigh she moved away from the window and looked down on what she was wearing—a skimpy black dress coupled with an inelegant Aran cardigan. She had no fear that Hugo Drake-Latimer would turn his charms on her. She hadn't a smidgen of Claudia's or Caroline's sophistication about her, and suddenly she was very tired and wished she were back in her hotel bedroom curled up in bed and listening to the owls hooting in the forest.

She heard the piano as soon as she opened her bedroom door to go downstairs, and it so took her by surprise that she leaned against the door-jamb and listened for a while. So it wasn't just for show—he did play, and so very well. Funny, but she would never have dreamt that he could play jazz—modern jazz, too. She would have put him down as a Chopin man. Strains of an Oscar Peterson melody drifted up and Angel was captivated.

When the keys finally stilled she went down to join him. He'd changed although she hadn't heard him moving about upstairs. Now he was relaxed in dark green cords and black polo-necked sweater. Less formal wear suited him just as well as a suit. He was pouring coffee, and already two brandies sat waiting on the sofa-table.

Angel moved into the room and he looked up and smiled at her. 'I made the choice for you—coffee to keep you awake long enough for the introductions, brandy to lull you to sleep in a strange house.'

'How thoughtful of you,' she murmured as she stood by the fire.

'Hugo—Hugo Drake-Latimer.' He stretched out his hand to her and she took it because it would be churlish not to. She didn't want him to know she already knew his name and what he was up to. She had no plan in mind but she didn't want to blow her chances yet.

'Angel—Angel Weston,' she told him fearlessly. She and Claudia were cousins through their mothers so their surnames were different. He would never know the connection between her and his last victim.

She took her hand from his because the contact was having a peculiar effect on her. His grip had been warm and strong and very pleasant and she hadn't expected that. She had always imagined felons to have cold, limp handshakes, though where she had got that idea from she didn't know. She'd never met a crook before.

He smiled and indicated for her to sit down, and she did, on the edge of the sofa with her legs primly posed. He slid back into a worn armchair by the side of the fire, looking relaxed and laid-back and at home—and that was, of course, because he was.

'Pretty name. Are you?'

'An angel?' She smiled thinly. 'I could fill a book of the names of men who've said that when they met me for the first time.'

'I suppose it was rather predictable,' he grinned. 'But what's your answer? I'm sure that's never predictable.'

'I'm usually polite rather than unpredictable. If I said I was an angel I'd have them *predictably* forecasting that they were the ones to change all that, and if I admitted I was far from angelic they would bay like hungry wolves.' She shrugged as she reached for her coffee. 'You can't win.'

'You sound world-weary, as if you have men pursuing you relentlessly.'

She grinned. 'I'm in the hotel business and hotels to men seem to hold aphrodisiac qualities. Once over the threshold they're pawing the ground like sex-starved wildebeest.'

To her astonishment he threw his head back and roared with laughter. When he'd finished and was lifting his brandy glass to his lips she wondered if she had struck a memory chord there. He and Claudia had met in a hotel bar.

'So, you get propositioned a lot, do you?'

'Only when I'm in the hotel itself, but most of the time I'm in the head-office penthouse.'

'Who do you work for?'

Angel gained time by sipping her coffee. She could use this to her advantage. If she answered his questions he'd think nothing of answering hers in return and she could find out all about him, and once armed with the information . . . then what? She didn't know, but something would come to her.

'The Railton Group. I'm secretary to Miles——'

'Wetherby,' he finished for her.

Angel nearly choked on her coffee. She slid the cup on to its saucer and reached for the brandy.

'You know him?' she breathed, wondering how well and wondering why she should be thrown by that revelation.

'Very well. We've done business together.'

'Oh.' Angel was shocked, not worried. So they had business connections? Miles was shrewd and surely wouldn't be deceived by this man, but Hugo Drake-Latimer hadn't said they were friends.

'So. . . so what sort of business are you in?' she asked bravely, though she knew.

'Oh, nothing that would interest you,' he threw casually back at her.

'Meaning I wouldn't understand?' she countered, bridling.

He looked at her through narrowed eyes. 'Meaning it would probably bore you to death.'

In other words, Mind your own business. But what he didn't know was that she already knew what sort of business he was in. Funny business under cover of an investment company. She had asked to avoid suspicion, and she would rather have heard it from his own mouth. One consolation, though, was that he hadn't immediately launched into his sales pitch, suggesting a phoney investment plan for her, as he had done with Claudia.

'And the crime writing?' Writers usually wrote what they knew and no doubt he had a few swindles to draw from.

'It's taking over my life,' he admitted, and didn't look too happy with that. 'It started out as a change from what I do all day and is gradually expanding upwards and outwards.'

'So what happens when you eventually get published?'

He smiled and offered her more brandy, which she declined with a shake of her head. Already she could feel a flush on her cheeks and the warmth was making her insides feel floaty.

'I am published,' he admitted quietly.

Vanity press, Angel guessed. He'd paid a publisher to print his work because if he hadn't she would have known and so would Claudia. But what Claudia had told Angel about the affair seemed to be limited to the emotional side of it rather than the practicalities. The affair had been a passionate one, and Angel supposed that when you were driven by heat and fire nothing else mattered.

So why had he never brought Claudia here? Claudia would have said, because this lovely cottage seemed built for romance...and crime, Angel reminded herself before the brandy floated her off to oblivion.

'You look tired,' he said quietly. 'I've phoned the hotel for you and told them you're safe here with me ynd you'll call tomorrow.' His eyes sparkled suddenly. 'Quite a tricky achievement as I didn't even know your name.'

Suddenly she was wide awake. 'You . . . you called the hotel?' How could she believe that? She wished she hadn't drunk that brandy because now she felt tense and stressed inside. She shouldn't be here, in this strange house with a strange man. No one knew she was here and no one would ever find her if . . . if . . .

He handed her the mobile phone and when she looked at him in puzzlement she saw a glint of anger in his eyes and wondered at that too.

'There's mistrust written all over your face, Angel,' he said coldly. 'Press the re-dial button and put your mistrust to bed and mellow out—I'm not out to fool you.' He stood up and picked up the coffee-pot from the sofa-table. 'I'll leave you alone to do it because it will be easier for you, and besides, I'd hate to witness your embarrassment when you find out I'm not a liar.'

He shut the door quietly behind him and Angel rather wished he'd slammed it because that would definitely have spurred her to plunge down the re-dial button on the receiver. Why did *he* make her feel guilty for doubting him?

To hell with him. She'd lie awake worrying all night if she didn't check him out. Without hesitation she plunged her forefinger on the re-dial button and listened to the clicks, then heard the receptionist at the White Swan answer in her nasal telephone voice. So he *had* called the hotel for her. She was about to ring off when it suddenly occurred to her that he might have called the number but not necessarily have spoken a word. She was getting quite accomplished at this detective lark.

'Angel Weston here,' she told the receptionist.

'Oh, Miss Weston, we were quite worried about you till Mr Drake-Latimer called and assured us you were in safe hands. What can I do for you?'

Angel thought quickly, whereas before she hadn't thought at all. Supposing she hadn't called Drake-Latimer's bluff and the receptionist hadn't heard from him this evening? But he had called and the receptionist sounded quite happy and it was Angel feeling awkward and ill at ease.

'I . . . I've left my travel alarm on. It's set for seven-thirty and I wouldn't want it to disturb anyone in the morning.' Phew! That had been an inspiration—and the truth, as it happened.

'No problem, Miss Weston, and thank you for being so thoughtful. The night porter will deal with it and we hope to see you back with us soon.'

And so do I, Angel thought despondently as she rang off and slammed the wretched phone down on the sofa beside her.

'I did call the hotel and spoke to the receptionist, who confirmed that you had rung,' she told Hugo as he came into the room with a fresh pot of coffee. 'I make no excuse for my doubts. I think they're quite reasonable and I won't apologise for them.'

'In that case I won't apologise for *my* doubts.' He leaned down and filled her coffee-cup with hot, fresh coffee.

'Your doubts?' Angel queried with indignation. 'How can you possibly doubt me? I'm a w——'

'Woman?' His eyes widened and Angel noticed his thick black eyelashes for the first time. 'And women these days are as devious as men. I don't for a minute believe your story of getting lost tonight. Without a doubt you followed me here and I won't push you at this late hour for a reason. You can tell me in your own good time. But seeing that you admitted to checking out my story with the hotel, I'll admit I ran my own check on you on the kitchen phone while I was making fresh coffee.'

'You did what?' Angel cried, struggling to her feet from the cosy warm depths of the sofa she had slid back into. He had slumped back into his armchair as cool as you like, whereas she would have preferred him on his feet to take her verbal onslaught face-on. 'How dare you run a check on me? How...what sort of a check, anyway?'

'Well, I have a few contacts in the police force——'

'The police!' Angel screeched. The nerve, from him of all people! You bet he had contacts: he probably had a string of convictions to his name and was known by the CID throughout the land.

'But I didn't use those, though I would have done if you hadn't checked out with Miles Wetherby.' His eyes were so dark and superciliously triumphant that Angel wanted to lunge at him.

'I...I don't believe you! You...you rang Miles...? You couldn't have done!'

'I did. More brandy?'

'No, I don't want any more brandy, or coffee, and how dare you embarrass me this way?' She dragged

her hand through her hair to clear it from her brow,
which was fiery with rage. 'How could you have done
that, and why, why, why?'

'I've told you why. You've acted very suspiciously
tonight and I don't trust you further than I can throw
you——'

Angel was incensed. 'Now just you listen to me!
I've no ulterior motives where you are concerned,
none whatsoever, and you have no reason to mistrust
me——'

'We could argue this point all night,' he interrupted, not rising in anger as she had done. His had
evaporated earlier when he had cooled off as he'd
made the second pot of coffee. 'It seems there is one
set of attitudes for women, another for men. Women
do assault men, you know, and blackmail them—even
murder them. Now, if this were your secret retreat
and I'd followed you home tonight, wouldn't you want
to run a check on me?'

'I already know...' Oh, hell, she could bite her
tongue off for that. Quick thinking was needed again.
'I already knew who you were,' she admitted in a
croaky whisper.

His eyes narrowed but he didn't say a word, because he was clever. He knew she wouldn't leave that
floating in the air. He'd have her digging her own grave
and jumping into it if she wasn't careful.

'I...I'd heard your name mentioned in the White
Swan and it...it rang a bell and then...then I saw
you...and I didn't know you but...really I was just
curious. It...it was probably why I stared at you like
that. I wasn't aware I was watching you but if you

say I did——' she shrugged '—then I must have done. Of course, now I know why I recognised your name, why it rang a bell. You know Miles, and he must have mentioned you—and it is rather an unusual name.'

Her whole body sagged and she sat down again on the sofa, saying a silent prayer for him to believe her, though she didn't deserve to have her prayers answered for telling such lies. She dared not look at him in case she saw disbelief in his eyes.

'Miles told me all I needed to know about you,' he said after a long pause.

Angel raised her head to look at him then. Why was she on trial here and not him? What a clever man he was.

'Am I permitted to know what he said, or have you some sort of gentlemen's agreement between you?'

'It's no secret,' he said with a shrug. 'He said you were the best secretary he'd ever had. Quietly efficient, always well turned out, intelligent and discreet, calm when all about you are under stress.'

'I sound as fascinating as a bag of broken biscuits,' Angel murmured into her coffee-cup.

She heard his soft laughter and gave him her attention again. He was smiling at her over the rim of his brandy glass. When he lowered it he spoke softly.

'That's his opinion, not mine—not that I would know if you were quietly efficient or not, but I could dispute your other talents.' His eyes raked over her now very creased black dress and the cardigan that had seen better days. 'You don't look very sharply dressed to me at the moment, and I'd hardly put you down as over-bright after the situation you've landed yourself in tonight. Discreet you are not—you've certainly added fuel to the gossip that will no doubt circulate the White Swan and surroundings now that they know you're staying the night in my cottage. And calm while under stress? It's a wonder your screams weren't heard in Kendal when I caught you in my front yard. If you ask my opinion I'd say the Angel Weston Miles Wetherby employs and holds dear to his heart doesn't fit the description of the lady sitting across from me now.'

Dear God, but he didn't believe she was who she was! This was totally unbelievable. He was the one who should be under the spotlight! She couldn't speak, she couldn't retaliate because she was...speechless. Eyes wide and mouth gaping, she watched him get to his feet and come across to her. To her utter surprise he reached down, took her firmly by the wrist and hauled her to her feet and...into his arms.

His mouth was suddenly hard on hers, so shockingly brutal that she was stunned for a moment, and then the most peculiar thing happened. She felt a shot of liquid fire sear through her, from the back of her neck right down to her toes. Her whole insides bucketed in a fury of delicious sensation which so astonished her that she went weak at the knees. Her body was rocked by a tingling and pulsing and as his grip tightened around her waist and he pulled her hard against his muscled power she thought her heart would give out with the pressure of her rushing blood.

He was aroused, and the thought that she had done that to him astonished her. But then a vision of

Claudia swam before her eyes—Claudia hysterical with grief over this man, Claudia weak and suffering from what he had done to her.

Angel tore her mouth from his, stepped back and her hand came up and swiped him hard across the face.

He didn't look one bit surprised or hurt, though she doubted her small hand had even caused a mild sensation on his skin. But the thought had been behind it and that was all that mattered. He smiled as his hand came up and he ruefully rubbed the side of his face.

'Now I know you're the real Angel Weston,' he drawled softly.

Angel stiffened and stared at him defiantly. 'And what exactly do you mean by that?' she blazed.

His eyes widened and he assessed her for a few seconds before saying, 'Can you take a bit of man talk?'

She didn't answer because she couldn't. Her throat was tight and sore and it wasn't in anticipation of what he might say. She was still suffering from the shock of that kiss and what it had done to her insides.

'"Angel pure, Angel bright, Angel unavailable, Angel white",' he recited softly.

Shocked and hurt, she stared at him with tears pricking the backs of her eyes. Miles couldn't have told him that: it was a penthouse joke, something between herself, Miles and his closest staff who worked on the top floor. But he *had* told him, that was obvious, and what was also obvious was that Hugo Drake-Latimer must be a very close friend of her employer because that sort of man talk only went between people who were close.

So if they were such good friends this . . . this con man couldn't be that bad, because Miles was so good.

Angel was confused and her confusion drew her back from him. She desperately tried to close him out of her mind because that kiss had registered something deep inside her and that was confusing too. She didn't know what was happening here.

'I'm . . . I'm going to bed,' she murmured, turning away from him, and he never said a word because he'd said it all already. He didn't trust her and that damned kiss had been a test of her morality, and thank heavens she'd had the nerve to slap him down before it had got out of hand.

CHAPTER THREE

THE bed was deliciously warm and welcome but sleep was hard to come by. Angel lay in the darkness listening to Hugo moving about in the bathroom and his bedroom. Later the only sound was of soft rain on the roof-tiles.

She couldn't believe all that had happened and that she was here in his cottage on this funny little island. He had been Claudia's lover, and yet somehow everything didn't jell. He didn't quite fit the image that Angel had formed of him. She could believe that he was an exciting lover, but the rest—a cold-hearted con man? But then the criminal mind was a mysterious one.

And Miles, knowing Hugo Drake-Latimer so well and telling him that rhyme about her. At this late hour Hugo must have phoned him at home, and Miles was such a very private person when he wasn't working that it had been further confirmation of their closeness. So how could Hugo Drake-Latimer be such a rat without Miles knowing?

But he hadn't been a rat to her, yet. In fact he had been quite nice in the circumstances. He'd checked her out and her first reaction had been indignation, but on second thoughts there was a lot of truth in what he'd said about equal rights. Or he could be naturally suspicious because of what he did to women.

45

Women? Did Angel know for sure that he had done to other women what he had done to Claudia? Tricked them out of their money and their hearts? It *appeared* that he had been doing that to Caroline, but she didn't know for sure.

Angel rolled over and punched the pillow hard. She had advised Claudia to go to the police but she had adamantly refused, saying that if she did that she'd never get him back. She still lived in the hope that it was all going to come out all right and he would come back to her. Angel slept on that bleak, improbable thought.

The pounding of tumultuous rain on the slate roof-tiles above her head woke her with a start the next morning. Angel sat bolt upright in bed, dazed but coming down to earth abruptly.

She skimmed her tousled hair from her face, rubbed her eyes, and when she looked her eyes focused on Hugo Drake-Latimer at the foot of the bed. In horror she snatched the sheet up to her chin. She was naked beneath it, and how long had he been standing there?

He held a mug of something in one hand, the other resting lightly on the pine footboard. He was smiling or grinning or leering—she wasn't sure which.

'Coffee?'

Angel held her hand out for it, flushed with embarrassment. 'Thanks,' she murmured and took it gratefully, hugging the sheet to her for comfort. She drew her knees up as he sat on the edge of the bed.

'It's still raining,' he told her quietly.

'My, you're sharp first thing in the morning,' she retorted, her sarcasm urged by the intimacy of the unnerving situation she had awoken to: Svengali at the foot of her bed.

The wind had changed and rain was now pounding incessantly at the windows, and with it came the realisation that no way was the water going to subside at this rate. Angel gulped at her coffee, relishing the new life it was bringing to her bones.

She looked at him over the rim of the mug and then lowered it, clutching it on her knees. She waited for him to say something. He did.

'Is it true—are you a virgin?' he asked quietly.

Angel responded the only way she could when confronted with such an unexpected question first thing in the morning. 'It's none of your business,' she told him coldly.

He shrugged. 'I know it isn't, but being a writer I'm madly curious about people, especially virgins.'

Angel raised a brow. He was an oddity, this man.

'Virgins feature a lot in your crime novels, do they?' she asked sarcastically.

'They're emotive characters in any novel,' he replied with a smile.

She leaned her head to one side and asked an absurd question she already knew the answer to. 'Are *you* a virgin?'

He grinned. 'Paying me back for last night?'

'Yes. You claim equal rights, why shouldn't I? Are you a virgin?'

'None of your business,' he countered.

Angel gave him a half-smile. 'So what prompted you to ask me such a loaded question? I don't believe for a minute you're gathering characters for another novel.'

'The poetry intrigued me. "Angel pure, Angel bright..."'

'Hardly poetry,' Angel muttered. She took a gulp of coffee and cradled the mug in her hands, which were wrapped round her knees. 'It was a joke. Well, not exactly a joke.' She sighed. 'We had a trainee manager once and he couldn't believe he wasn't God's gift to women. He couldn't believe I wouldn't go out with him either. One morning I came into the office and that little piece of "poetry" was on everyone's computer screen. A man scorned and all that. Miles sacked him.'

'Miles must think a lot of you.'

Angel looked at him from under thick lashes, her eyes sparkling. 'Miles sacked him because he was a bloody awful trainee manager.'

Hugo grinned and there was a long pause before either spoke, giving Angel time to consider her position. Here she was, sitting naked in bed, nursing a mug of coffee that Hugo Drake-Latimer had made for her. She'd spent a night in his cottage and she had said things to him that she wouldn't have dreamt of saying to Patrick. He was a crook and a womaniser, had driven her cousin into a depression and she should be hating him to the very soles of his shoes. Instead she found him...well...fascinating, and she supposed that was where the danger lay—in allowing her resistance to be lowered far enough for him to slide into her confidence. Lady, beware, she told herself.

She forced herself to speak because his penetrating eyes were making her feel uncomfortable again. 'Silly question, but I don't suppose the water has gone down enough for me to get off this island?'

He shook his dark head. 'Could be days.'

'I'm due back at work in five.'

'Miles will understand if it's longer.' He stood up and took the mug from her fingers. 'Ready for breakfast?'

'I've no clothes,' she uttered helplessly.

He nodded towards the wardrobe across the room. 'Take your pick. Laura won't mind and you look about the same size.'

Angel stared up at him, her heart bleeping for some reason. 'Laura?' she repeated in a dull voice. He *was* married. His wife had left him—no, she was away for a few days...with the children!

He read her uncertainty and smiled knowingly. 'Laura, my sister. She takes her holidays here a couple of times a year.'

'And has enough clothes to keep a second wardrobe here?' Angel exclaimed in disbelief, at the same time suffering a tiny pang of envy for the excess clothes and the holidays.

'She likes to travel light.'

She didn't know whether to believe him or not. But how could she when she knew all about him?

'I don't like wearing other people's clothes,' she stated flatly.

He gave her a shrug. 'I'm sorry but I can't offer you anything else. Have you ever worn anyone else's clothes?'

'Of course not,' she retorted.

'How do you know you don't like it, then?'

'It's the thought,' Angel protested, giving a small shudder.

He leaned towards her. 'Don't think about it, then.'

'I won't, because I'm not going to do it,' she fired back. 'I'll wear my little black dress and...and...'

He held a hand up to silence her. 'I'm really not bothered, lovely. If you change your mind——'

'I won't!'

She did, though, five minutes after he left the room, when she picked her dress up from the floor where it had lain crumpled all night. She had hung it over the back of a chair and it had slid off...damn him!

His sister had taste at least—even her jeans were designer and most of the clothes were in dry cleaner's polythene, so why not?

'You changed your mind, then?' he said, trailing his eyes over the blue jeans and baggy grey lambs-wool sweater she was wearing.

They fitted her perfectly and she wondered if she reminded him of his sister; for a reason she didn't understand, she hoped not.

'Obviously,' she uttered as she sat down at the small kitchen table in the middle of the room.

Hugo cleared his throat as he turned from the grill where he was frizzling bacon.

Angel flushed hotly and jumped to her feet. 'I'm sorry. Is there anything I can do?'

He looked relieved. 'Yes, make some fresh coffee, or tea if you prefer. And pop some toast in the toaster and get a couple of eggs out of the fridge and——'

'And shall I do the breakfast?' Angel huffed in resignation.

His eyes brightened and he beamed. 'Good girl. I need to make some calls.'

Angel opened her mouth to protest and closed it again as he abandoned the grill and went out of the door. She'd asked for all this, she told herself as she rescued the bacon. Yes, it was all her own fault. She should have minded her own business and kept out of it. It was Claudia's problem, not hers, and it was a pity she hadn't thought of that sooner instead of imagining herself a female Mickey Spillane.

'It's ready,' she called out when she had dished up the breakfast.

'You're quite a treasure,' he complimented as he sat down to his breakfast.

Angel sat across from him thinking that 'treasure' wasn't a word she liked to be described by.

'You make me sound like a lady that *does* for a man.' As soon as she said it she wished she'd phrased that better.

His grin and the shaking of his head showed he thought the same thing, but he didn't say anything.

'Do you expect me to cook all the meals while I'm here?'

He sliced through his bacon and then looked up at her. 'I don't expect anything of you, Angel, but don't forget I could have turned you out last night.'

'Don't try to appeal to my conscience——'

'Haven't you one, then?'

'Not where you're concerned,' she bit back. 'Yes, I appreciate that you needn't have given me shelter last night, that you could have left me to sleep in my car or, worse, made me go back the way I had come, and yes, I'm grateful but not——'

'Grateful enough to look after my needs in return?' he suggested.

The way he locked his eyes into hers after he said that left Angel in no doubt what he meant. Surprisingly her insides didn't recoil in horror at the very thought. In fact the slight turbulence she felt inside was miles removed from horror.

'As you're a friend of my boss, I trust you not to push your intentions where they are not wanted,' she said rather primly. 'More coffee?'

She lifted the pot, he held his cup up and she poured without the slightest tremor. 'I'll cook for you,' she told him charitably. 'There'll be precious little else for me to do while I'm here. Dishwasher?' She looked around and there was one next to the sink. 'Good. I foresee no problems.'

'Don't you now?' he muttered under his breath as he forked a slice of grilled tomato.

Angel glared at him. 'I know what you're thinking, you know. You think it could be a problem, us under the same roof. Well, I don't. It doesn't bother me one bit because my feet are firmly on the ground.'

'And you've obviously been reading too many romances lately.'

'I beg your pardon?'

He smiled across at her and gave a slight shrug of his shoulders. 'I've not said a word, Angel, lovely. You're the one doing all the protesting about us coping together under the same roof. I'm not after your body, delicious as it is——'

'You made a pass at me last night,' Angel protested hotly. 'You actually kissed me and then, this very morning, you asked if...' Her voice trailed to a dead end and her eyes narrowed. 'What do you mean, "delicious as it is"?' He sounded as if he had seen her body. Surely he hadn't spied on her when she had been flitting around the bedroom deciding what to wear?

'Your body. It *is* quite delicious, what I saw of it.'

He *had* been spying on her.

He smiled at her, one of those sparkly smiles, and he leaned across the table as if about to divulge a confidence. His voice was low and seductive. 'Angel, you have the most beautiful breasts I have ever seen——'

Shocked, Angel nearly choked. She shot to her feet, but before she could flee the kitchen his hand shot out and caught her wrist and he swung her round till she landed full on his lap with a squeal.

His mouth was a fraction of an inch from her ear, his breath warm on it.

'You really must learn how to take compliments, Angel. Especially from me. I don't give them away freely.'

Angel struggled but he held her firmly. 'It's no compliment knowing that a man spies on a woman when she's dressing!' she blurted hotly.

'Now why should I need to resort to spying while you dress when awakening you is *such* a revealing pleasure?' he drawled teasingly.

The colour flushing her face deepened. How long had he been standing at the foot of her bed this morning?

'I see no difference in spying while I dress or spying while I wake. You should have knocked!'

'I did; you answered——'

'I did not!'

'You did. Slightly dazed, but you said a definite "come in" and come in I did. And there you were, sitting up in bed, rubbing your eyes and deliciously naked from the waist up.'

Angel went to twist out of his grasp but there was no need to struggle. He let her go with a soft, teasing laugh.

'And you do have the most beautiful——'

'Shut up!'

Angel sat down across from him and feverishly slicked a slice of toast with marmalade.

'No butter?' he teased softly.

Angel slammed her knife down and glared at him. 'It's your fault. You completely unnerve me and it's why I'm so dead against spending time here. Damn the rain! Damn you! You've kissed me, you've asked me if I'm a virgin, you've seen me half naked. I don't even know you, and so far you know more about me than my boyfriend!'

She proceeded to scrape the marmalade off the toast and daub it with butter this time. Then on went the marmalade again and she bit into it before he spoke again.

'A boyfriend, eh? One who's never told you your breasts are beautiful?'

Angel stopped chewing and stared at him in disbelief. Never had she met anyone quite like him. The comparison with Patrick, she supposed, was inevitable. Patrick didn't talk like this.

She swallowed. 'No, he hasn't,' she told him quietly and defensively. 'Patrick has more important things on his mind than the state of my breasts!'

'Patrick, eh? Irish, is he?'

'From Irish stock, yes.'

'Hmm. I've always found the Irish to be passionately romantic.'

Angel concentrated on pouring herself some more coffee. Was he implying that Patrick wasn't? She supposed he could be right. It was funny, but she had never considered it before—that Patrick wasn't romantic. He was nice, though... Angel found her thoughts floundering. Was love nice?

'Is Caroline your girlfriend?' she asked brazenly. Why should he be the only one allowed to probe?

He laughed. 'Caroline, eh? You *were* eavesdropping very hard last night in the restaurant.'

Angel couldn't meet his eye. 'Is she your girlfriend?' she insisted, and made heavy weather of adding sugar to her coffee to cover her embarrassment.

'I much prefer talking about you.'

Of course, a crook like him wouldn't want to give anything away about himself. It was the first time for about half an hour that she had thought of him as a crook again, and that was a salutary lesson. She should be telling herself he was a crook and a womaniser *all* the time!

'You have the advantage over me. You ran a check on me last night and found out far more about me than I would be willing to tell you, and yet you aren't willing to tell me anything about yourself. I just want to even things up a bit.'

'Why, do you think we have something going?'

Astonished, she gasped at him again and then decided she had better get used to this, his openness.

'I don't, but you obviously think so.'

To her dismay he shook his head. 'My main interest in you stems from wild curiosity...'

Angel took a tighter grip on her coffee-cup. So he didn't fancy her. She wouldn't lose sleep over it.

'At the moment,' he added quietly.

Angel's insides tensed.

'When I've fathomed you out I'll allow myself to think of other things, but until then I shall act with extreme caution,' he concluded, the narrowing of his dark eyes testifying to that.

'You didn't last night—you kissed me.' She wasn't going to let him get away with all this nonsense.

He smiled thinly. 'You were such a temptation and it was also part of my character analysis.'

'Character analysis? I'm not going to be in your next novel, am I?'

'Not unless you commit a terrible crime.'

Angel started to gather up the dirty dishes. 'That's always a possibility,' she said staunchly. 'You're enough to drive anyone to crime and, talking of which, is it necessary to have a criminal mind to be able to write crime novels?'

Perhaps this was a way of finding out why he had done such a thing to Claudia. The trouble was she wasn't a psychiatrist and she wouldn't be able to analyse his reply whatever he said.

'One needs to have a devious mind.'

'Does one?' she uttered under her breath as she turned to the dishwasher. Well, that was confirmation at least. He had a devious mind. 'So, if I'm not to appear in one of your books, why the character analysis?'

'Because you intrigue me.' He got up and came to her, handing her the dishwasher liquid from a cupboard under the sink. 'You don't run true to form and that interests me.'

Angel paused from slotting the knives and forks in the cutlery basket. 'Go on,' she urged quietly. Now she was madly curious to know why she interested him so. It could be that he was sizing her up to be his next victim. It could be that she could *pretend* to fall for his tricks and so expose him!

'Well, what have I got so far?' he mused as he leaned back against the work surface. 'A conscientious worker, according to her employer. A supposed virgin... I'm not sure about that yet. Certainly someone choosy about her boyfriends, picking safety rather than passion. A bit of a prude where her nakedness is concerned, which suggests she hasn't yet discovered her own sensuality——'

'Just a minute!' Angel interrupted hotly. 'This isn't a character analysis, it's a character *assassination*!'

He eyed her darkly. 'I haven't finished yet. Where was I?'

'Putting down my sexuality by the sound of it,' she cried despondently.

His eyes widened mockingly. 'Aha,' he breathed. 'This is getting more interesting than ever. Are you indignant about my analysing your sexuality and possibly coming up with the wrong conclusions?' he quizzed smoothly.

'What are you?' Angel retorted scornfully. 'Some sort of lay Freud?'

He laughed. 'Yes, he was rather obsessed with the libido.'

Angel flushed, realising what she had said. 'I didn't mean that. Anyway, where is all this leading?'

'Hopefully to finding out why a beautiful young Angel, blind to her own sexuality, a conventional sort of career girl with a steady boyfriend, a girl who is quietly domesticated, certainly not a feminist, a moral girl, possibly a virgin, follows a strange man to an off-the-beaten-track hotel, watches him intently through dinner, then calmly hops into her car and follows him to his secret hideaway *and* manipulates her way into spending a few days with him.'

Angel stared at him in disbelief, her heart crashing around inside her so chaotically that she thought it would fail at any second. She had honestly believed he had accepted her excuses. Oh, he was shrewd and smart and . . . and devious. He had a point, though. She had acted out of character. Not at all like the

Angel Weston who was considering marrying quiet, safe Patrick. So how could she get out of admitting the truth—that she knew him to be the man who had broken her cousin's heart and swindled her out of her fortune and *that* was why she had followed him?

'So, what have you to offer me, Angel?' he asked very softly.

Angel very carefully shut the door of the dishwasher and set it in motion. A very deliberate act to steady her own nerves. She didn't know what to say. Her throat was dry and so were her lips and she couldn't have spoken if she had known what to say.

'Shall I make an attempt at trying to analyse you further?' he suggested quietly. When she still made no reply he went on, 'I think you have a personality problem at the moment, more than likely born of your fear of ending up with the wrong man.'

Angel looked up from the wash cycle of the machine she had been studying intently. Her eyes were as wide as one of the saucers she'd just loaded, her heart swishing like the washing-up water.

'I... I don't understand,' she whispered.

'Of course you don't and that's why you're acting out of character and not even realising what you're doing. Tell me, is it a serious relationship with Patrick?'

'Look, this is ridiculous!' Angel protested. 'My life has nothing to do with you!'

'But it has everything to do with me at the moment. You are here, in my life, under my roof. I didn't ask you. You were the one that chose to barge into my world. I'm just trying to understand why.'

'I told you last night. I got lost and——'

'You were looking for some adventure in your life.'

Angel made a snorting noise. 'You're crazy. Most writers are, crime writers probably more so than others. Did Humpty Dumpty fall off the wall or was he pushed? You just have an unnaturally suspicious mind. Why on earth should I be looking for adventure in my life?'

'Because you're stuck in a rut with Patrick,' he said quietly, and his eyes met hers and were so intent that they defied her to argue.

This man was so frank and so chillingly near the truth. Angel saw it now and suspected that she had seen it coming but hadn't wanted to admit it. Yes, she had acted out of character in coming here to the Lakes on her own for a few days' break, and it was probably because she needed her own space to think. But she hadn't actually *thought* much about Patrick because chance had taken over back at the White Swan, pure chance in the form of running into her cousin's one-time lover.

Angel ran a hot tongue over hot lips, lifted her chin and turned her head to face him.

'If I am in a rut it's a very comfortable one,' she told him truthfully.

'And that's what you want, is it? Comfort and security?'

Angel lowered her eyes. 'I . . . I suppose it's what every woman wants.'

She felt his fingers under her chin and it was an electrifying sensation, far removed from comfort and security and far removed from any sensation she had experienced with Patrick.

'No, it isn't what every woman wants, Angel. Shall I tell you what you'll get if you marry this man?'

Angel parted her moist lips and uttered softly, 'He hasn't asked me to marry him yet.'

Hugo formed a very small smile on his lips. 'He will. If he has an ounce of sense in his body he will, but, whereas he will be happy in his comfortable marital rut, you won't, my lovely.'

Angel could hardly bear the sensation of his thumb caressing her chin, and when it moved to run tenderly across her lower lip she thought she would melt to the ground in a blob.

'You want fire and passion and a man to sweep you off your feet...'

She opened her mouth to protest but his thumb prevented the utterance of any heated words she might form.

'The trouble is you don't know it,' he went on smoothly, 'and the trouble is I'm very tempted to prove my character analysis to be true. Trouble is I'm not sure if that would be the only reason. Trouble is I think I'm heading for trouble.'

He lowered his head and held hers firmly with the hand that had lifted her chin and run crazily over her lower lips. Now his lips ran crazily over hers and the sensation was complete and utter bliss.

She couldn't move, though. She couldn't respond or move away or even breathe. His warmth and sensuality blitzed her being till she felt dizzy and hot and so very certain of how deeply Claudia had felt for this man. Angel could feel herself falling under his spell. Maybe she already had, because she was making no attempt to stop his hands sliding around her waist and pulling her hard against the length of his body.

She could feel his muscled power, hear his own heart thudding in time with hers, smell his masculinity and . . . and it was delicious. A sensation so heady and powerful and . . . and sexual.

His mouth moved more ardently, parting her lips and tasting her inner sweetness, and then she knew what fire and passion were and she knew that this was the first time she had ever experienced them. It was like nothing else. It was like nothing she had ever had with Patrick.

He drew back from her at last and his breath was as uneven and ragged as hers, and for one glorious moment she almost convinced herself that he was as deeply moved by the experience as she was. But he had the advantage over her. He had the advantage of experience over naïveté. He'd done all this with others. He'd done all this with Claudia. He'd lowered her resistance with the potency of his sexuality and, when she was at her weakest and most vulnerable, poached her fortune and left her wondering what had hit her.

And then Angel knew that trouble had hit her too. She had no money so he couldn't take that from her, but she had a heart—and how easily she could lose it to this enigma of a man.

'The next move is yours, Angel,' he murmured against her lips, brushing a tantalising kiss across her mouth. 'You choose how far and deep you want to plunge into the depths of passion.'

Her hands came up to his chest and she held him firmly away from her. Her heart was ricocheting around her ribcage at his suggestion that from now on she should take the initiative. She wouldn't do that, not ever. She couldn't; it wasn't in her.

'I think you could be very wrong about that rut you think I'm out of place in,' she whispered. 'At the moment it appeals far more than the risk of an affair with a man who wants to prove that his characterisation is spot-on.'

He smiled and his grip tightened very slightly around her narrow waist. 'Angel pure, Angel bright, I think I'm beginning to fall in love with you.'

Love! Oh, no, Angel couldn't and *wouldn't* swallow that one. This was all an act, part of his deception ploy. He'd probably said those very words to Claudia to lull her into a false sense of security. He probably said it to *all* his victims.

Then his mouth covered hers again, so sweetly, so wonderfully sensually that a lesser person than herself would have succumbed immediately. But Angel pure, Angel bright hadn't just fallen off the Christmas tree because she had just discovered something new about herself. Yes, he was right—she craved passion and adventure and fire in her life, but a cheap con man wasn't the one to satisfy the hunger just because he thought he had discovered it for her. It had been there all the time and had just needed nudging awake. No, the something new she had discovered about herself

was that she was a tougher nut to crack than Claudia.
But, she admitted, she had hindsight to help her—
not that she needed any help to ward Hugo Drake-
Latimer off. She was quite capable of coping with the
task herself . . . Yes, quite capable.

CHAPTER FOUR

HUGO'S smile was as enigmatic as his character. It seemed that he knew what she was thinking. But of course he could never know that Angel knew the truth about him.

He let his hands drop from her waist and when he spoke it was as if the last few minutes had never happened.

'So how can I entertain you while you're here?'

There was no hint of double meaning and Angel felt a small pull of disappointment at her heart-strings. Her sensibility rebelled at the sensation. Here she was convinced she could cope with all this and her heart was betraying her already.

'Don't worry about me. I'll keep myself occupied if you want to work. I'll . . . I'll bake a cake.'

A sardonic black brow rose like a raven's wing ready for flight. 'I doubt you'll find a cake-tin among my kitchen equipment,' he told her.

Angel felt her cheeks colouring. How stupid of her. He was a bachelor, a crook, a womaniser . . . She bit her lip and shrugged.

'I'll *think* about making one, then. That should keep me occupied for an hour or so. It will have to be a fruit-cake, though.'

Hugo laughed. '*You're* the fruit-cake. What about a book to read?'

'Your own?'

'Never. I couldn't stand the tension of wondering what you were thinking of it. I have a small library you can browse through before I get down to work. Laura might have left a few romantic novels lying around. She adores them.'

Angel followed him out into the hallway. He obviously thought her a dreamer at heart like his sister and . . . and who was to say he wasn't right? She had done some dreamy things in the last couple of days.

She hadn't noticed the other door opening off the hallway before. Hugo was already in the room and Angel followed. It was a lovely room. A coal fire crackled in the grate of a redbrick fireplace. The walls were lined with books and by the window, on a desk, was a word processor. There was a worn armchair with a multicoloured patchwork quilt thrown over it by the fireside, a tapestry-covered footstool and a brass fender.

'It's a lovely study,' she murmured. 'You obviously take your hobby seriously.'

He gave her a wry smile and switched on his computer. 'I've lit the fire in the sitting-room for you.'

Angel felt that she was being dismissed. She glanced quickly over the bookshelves to make her selection; she would have appreciated more time because it was going to be a long day and she didn't want to be stuck with a book she couldn't enjoy.

'Take your time,' he told her as he picked up a computer disk and examined it.

He was so astute. He could read her like a book!

'Oh, I haven't read this!' she exclaimed, sliding a hardback out from a row of books by the same author. 'Hetty D. Lang—you like her too?' She smiled to herself, somehow pleased that they shared the same taste in thrillers. 'It's funny, isn't it, how good women are at writing in what you would think would be a male-dominated genre?'

She glanced across at him and felt a blush forming. He stood leaning back on the desk by the window and he was smiling.

'I'm sorry,' she said quickly. 'No offence, you being a budding crime writer and all that.' She fiddled with the book in her hand, turning it over to read the blurb on the back but the blurb was a blur. She hadn't meant to put him down in any way. She imagined writers to have very tender egos.

'That's her latest,' he said quietly. 'It's not even released yet.'

Angel's head shot up and her eyes widened. 'Oh, do you know her?'

No answer came, just another of his enigmatic smiles, and then suddenly she knew. She coloured furiously, and her heart hammered so loudly that she thought he must be able to hear it in the stillness of his study.

Suddenly his computer bleeped its impatience at being left unattended, and he turned and slotted a disk in. Angel, wide-eyed and astonished, stared at the back of his head. *He* was Hetty D. Lang? No, surely not. He couldn't be.

He turned back to her.

'Are you?' she breathed heavily.

'Am I what?'

'You can't be—I mean...' H.D.L. Hetty D. Lang, Hugo Drake-Latimer. Yes, he must be, but Claudia had never said and she would have done if she had known! '*Are* you... did you write these books?'

He folded his arms across his chest. 'You sound totally amazed, as if the very idea is unthinkable. Men do write under women's names occasionally, you know.'

'I know,' she uttered weakly, so shocked that she could hardly believe it. 'But Cl——' She stopped. Oh, no, she had nearly let Claudia's name slip out; if she had, all would have been lost. She swallowed and turned the book over in her hand, staring at it again. 'They're going to make a television series out of them,' she breathed. She'd read that just recently.

She lifted her head and looked at him again. He'd make a lot of money out of that. He'd probably made a lot of money out of these books already, so what on earth was he up to, swindling wealthy divorcees out of their fortunes?

'Yes,' he murmured. 'I signed the contract only last week.'

'But I thought... I mean, you led me to believe it wasn't a big thing, just something you did for a hobby.'

'I said I was published.'

'You didn't say to what extent. You said it was almost taking over your life but I didn't think... I mean, how on earth do you find the time? Your investment company...' Her heart nearly stopped.

He frowned slightly. 'I don't recall telling you I was in investments.'

Angel went hot inside. 'Miles did,' she said quickly, hoping he'd believe her and not run another check on her with her boss. 'And besides, you said you'd done business with Miles and . . . and I assumed it to be investments. How...how do you combine the two?' she asked, eager to divert the conversation away from how she knew.

'Not very well, I'm afraid,' he admitted with a shrug. 'I confess to delegating quite a bit recently. I'd much rather be here writing than locked in an office suite with my investors but——' he shrugged again '—my father's a Lloyd's underwriter and I grew up in a money-orientated environment and, well, that's the way it goes.'

His father a Lloyd's underwriter? That was serious money, and he was in investments *and* a successful author. Surely he couldn't be the same man who had deceived Claudia? She dredged her mind for more information, little things that Claudia had told her about her one-time lover. He was a passionate man, Claudia had emphasised that; she'd positively thrilled at recalling to Angel just how passionate he was. Well, so far that was the only thing that cross-matched with this Hugo Drake-Latimer. Now Angel knew for herself just how passionate he was. But little else but the name fitted the womanising pirate, and yet . . . and yet she had witnessed for herself him giving some advice to that Caroline in the hotel restaurant. Oh, hell, she didn't know at all, she really didn't.

'Are you sure you want to read it?'

She was so deep in her thoughts that she had forgotten she was clutching his book.

'Do you mind?'

'I don't if you don't, but usually I don't like people close to me reading my books. Writers can reveal a lot about themselves without knowing it.'

She felt flattered that he thought of her as someone close to him, but surely she should be cautious instead? He was getting far too close to her for comfort and not only because he had said he was falling in love with her. That was just a part of his scheme of things and so was this intimacy. But why, why did this man resort to such lowly cheating? He had money enough surely? But perhaps it went deeper than that. He was a crime writer, wasn't he? Maybe that was how he did his research, from personal experience!

'I would like to read it,' she told him. 'I've ... I've enjoyed all the others.'

He leaned across his desk and took a couple of books down from the shelf beside it. 'Here, take these as well in case you change your mind.'

In other words, Don't come disturbing me if you get bored. She took the books and thanked him. They were historical romances, just the sort she liked.

'Shall I make you lunch later?'

He'd turned back to his word processor and was scrolling through files, and she thought he hadn't heard her.

'Shall I ... ?'

'No, no. I don't expect it of you, but...' He sounded vague and offhand.

'But if there's a spare bacon sandwich going, don't hesitate to bring it in,' she muttered under her breath as she went to the door.

'Angel?'

She turned at the door and he was smiling at her. 'Thank you, that would be nice.'

She smiled back and shut the door behind her; her heart was hammering again and she wished he wouldn't be so nice because he *wasn't* nice. He had nearly broken Claudia's heart!

Angel went upstairs and made her bed before she did anything else. She wondered if she ought to make his too but decided against it. For one thing his bedroom was over the study and the floorboards in this old cottage could do with some oiling, and she didn't want him to think she was being nosy. The trouble was that if she dared to go into his room she wouldn't be able to stop herself being nosy. And if he caught her having a snoop... She shuddered at the thought.

And what would she be looking for—evidence? Angel went downstairs and made coffee. What sort of evidence? She really wasn't into this amateur detective work.

I want to forget it, she suddenly realised. I don't want to think of him as Claudia's lover and the man who cheated her. It was a sobering thought because it immediately posed a question. How far would she be willing to let herself go with her emotions with this man if she didn't know what he had done to Claudia?

She took him a mug of coffee. She said nothing, but moved silently and placed it next to him; he said nothing and she knew he was in another world. She shut the door noiselessly behind her and felt an odd feeling of emptiness inside her, as if he had shut her out of his life. It was silly because she wasn't even in his life.

Angel curled up on the sofa in front of the log fire he had lit for her. She had her coffee, she was gloriously warm and cosy and she had a good book, what more could she want? She stared into the fire. Something was missing and she suspected it was him.

Determinedly she picked up his book and started to read.

'That bad, is it?'

Angel woke with a start. She swung her legs from the sofa and the book thudded to the floor. He picked it up and sat down beside her, let the book open naturally and started to read from that page.

'Come one step closer and I'll blast you to hell and back!' he read.

Angel snatched the book from him. 'You didn't write that!' she cried.

'Perhaps I should have done,' he said with a grin. 'It might have kept you awake.'

'I wasn't bored...I mean, the book isn't boring...'

'But you couldn't keep your eyes open. Don't apologise——'

'I wasn't going to,' she interjected quickly. 'I was going to try and explain.'

He raised a brow and she went on, 'I couldn't get into it.'

'Oh, dear,' he murmured, but she knew he wasn't hurt.

'I couldn't get into it because I couldn't detach myself. I mean, I know you, and I've never read a book written by someone I know. I kept thinking and wondering——'

'And that's why I wasn't too keen on you reading it. I don't actually do those murders, you know.'

Angel smiled and looked down at the rug at her feet. 'I know, but as I said, it's a strange new experience for me, reading a book written by someone I know.'

'You hardly know me.'

True, she hardly knew him, only what she knew from Claudia, which was all bad and a contradiction of what she had found for herself.

'Yes, I hardly know you and yet we've shared some intimacies that I haven't shared with any other writer—not that I know any—so it makes a difference.' She was suddenly aware that his arm had crept along the back of the sofa.

'Like kissing, you mean?'

She might have guessed he'd come up with something like that. She stood up and picked her coffee-mug up from the floor.

'I'll make some lunch.'

He stood up with her. 'I'll help you. I fancy an omelette. OK with you?'

They ate in the kitchen, and then Hugo excused himself to get back to his work and Angel cleared up, feeling that strange loss once again. Married life with him could be miserable, with him locked away in his study all day. She shrugged. But it was no different from him going out to work at a nine-to-five job... Heavens! What on earth was she thinking? Imagining a life with him... a married life!

Later Angel piled logs on the fire in the sitting-room and then went back to the kitchen to plan an evening meal. The rain was relentless and the mist seemed to cling all around the cottage. The garden was scarcely visible through the kitchen window. Just a few ghostly shrubs penetrated the gloom, dripping with cold moisture. A wall of mist obscured anything beyond. It was like living in a vacuum. There was a world out there but to Angel it didn't exist. It was probably like that for Hugo, all the time he was steeped in his writing.

Angel stared out at the mist and knew that he had made some sort of impact on her life, and in such a short time, which was even more astonishing. She *wanted* to be here; even knowing what she knew she wanted to be here. That was the power of the man, the danger of him, and that was a danger to herself. She had Patrick and was probably going to marry him, and that comfortable rut she predicted was right for her. Danger she didn't need.

Hugo's freezer was well-stocked and Angel found chicken breasts, defrosted them in the microwave and left them in a marinade of garlic and herbs. She plundered his fruit bowl and made a fresh-fruit salad, and knew that as she worked she was fired by the need to please him.

'You can't marry this Patrick, you know,' he told her later as they ate in the kitchen. 'You're far too good a cook.'

Angel half smiled and ladled some more chicken casserole on to his plate. 'That's a funny way of giving me a compliment. Couldn't you have just said I was a good cook without bringing Patrick into it?'

'The intention wasn't to compliment you on your cooking, though that was an added bonus for you. It was more a warning really. Don't do it.'

'Marry Patrick?'

'You don't love him.'

'I do.'

'Not enough, then.'

'You don't know me, and besides he hasn't asked me yet, and if and when he does your warnings will make no difference to my decision at all.'

He smiled mysteriously. 'Maybe it won't be my warnings that will change your mind at the eleventh hour; maybe it will be the excitement I've brought into your life.'

Angel laughed. 'What excitement?'

'Don't you find being here an excitement in itself?' He leaned back, waiting for an answer, twirling his wine glass on the linen tablecloth Angel had unearthed from a kitchen drawer on her meanderings around his kitchen as she had prepared the dinner.

Wild horses wouldn't drag from her the truth that, yes, she did find it exciting. It was probably the most exciting thing she had ever done in her life, following this man to his secret lake hideaway, and it would be the last. Cooking dinner for him had given her a chance to think, really think. He was a very attractive man but way over her head. He was too complex for her. The man had a criminal mind, he practised fraud and wrote about crime, he played jazz superbly and with feeling, and he kissed like . . . like no one she had ever kissed before.

'I find being here . . . different,' she said at last, and just managed to meet his gaze across the top of her own wine glass. 'It's a bit of an odd happening.'

'An odd happening,' he repeated, rolling the words around his mouth. He smiled. 'I like odd happenings.'

'Because you're odd yourself,' Angel muttered as she cleared the dishes.

'Am I?' he said, starting to help himself from the dish of fruit salad. 'Then so are you,' he added softly.

She sat down, and he slid a full bowl across for her and smiled. 'There's a programme I want to see on Channel Four. Would you mind if we ate this in the sitting-room?'

'You go ahead. I'll make the coffee and bring it through.'

Angel sat in the kitchen after he had gone and stared at the fruit she couldn't eat. How could he be so *normal* and yet so complex?

'I hope you don't mind,' she started when the advertisements were on, 'but I called the hotel again. I thought I ought to tell them I probably couldn't make it for a few days. I also felt I ought to offer them some sort of an explanation.' As she spoke she was pouring coffee. She handed him his. 'I told them I worked for a magazine and that I was doing an article about you and because of the weather——'

'And I told them you were a distant cousin from New Zealand, looking up Brit relatives——'

The telephone buzzed and it cut into the definite buzz in Angel's head as she remembered the receptionist's change of tone when she had started her explanation. She must have thought Angel totally mad, and she must have thought that two very different explanations for her absence from the hotel were decidedly suspicious. She probably thought the very worst!

Hugo picked up the phone from a side-table, and almost immediately stood up and took himself and the phone out of the room, closing the door firmly behind him.

A call he didn't want overheard? Angel flew to the door and listened, feeling no qualms about doing it either.

'I'm sorry, Caroline. I completely forgot to call you. I'm stranded here again ... No, not bored, though I would be if I weren't well into the latest book. Yes, it's going well ... Oh, I'm glad you came round to my way of thinking. It's for the best ... You won't regret it, I promise you. I'll set it in motion for you. Of course, darling, yes, yes, I promise. Yes, it is a nuisance but hopefully the rain will cease overnight and I'll be free to get over...'

Angel didn't hear his goodbyes but she knew they would be syrupy. Caroline was the sort to demand syrupy goodbyes and, because he was on to a winner, he would deliver.

'Caroline,' he said as he came back into the room.

Angel was on her knees furiously jamming another log on the fire. So he'd be bored if it weren't for his writing. She felt stung.

She sat back on her heels and looked up at him. 'You didn't have to tell me that.'

He frowned. 'I know I didn't, but I thought it polite to tell you after I left the room so abruptly.'

'And why did you leave the room so abruptly? Terrified I might sneeze or something and give the game away?' She couldn't help sounding scathing.

He smiled knowingly and sat down on the sofa, picked up the remote control of the television and started zapping through the channels. He *was* bored.

'Yes. I didn't want her to know you were here. I doubt if she would have accepted the story you've spun me. She would have thought I was here with a lover——'

'And would have been madly jealous!' Angel blurted. She was stinging inside. Stinging to think he had kissed her the way he had, all the time having Caroline in his heart. He really was an evil man and she was in so much danger of falling for him!

Hugo looked at her directly and she almost lost her nerve and looked away, but this was the only way to deal with him, with the same directness he used.

'Yes, she probably would have been madly jealous,' he told her evenly.

'So she *is* your lover,' she challenged, her eyes darkening.

'Does it matter?'

Be careful, Angel warned herself inwardly. She was very much in danger here of making a complete fool of herself.

'It matters as much as your warnings about my boyfriend matter to me.'

'Oh, dear, for a glorious moment I thought you might be jealous,' he teased.

With iron reserve Angel got up from the hearthrug and poured more coffee. She had been jealous; for one tiny, minuscule fraction of a millionth of a second she *had* been jealous! But why? Why, when she knew him to be a thief of hearts? Why, when she had a future with Patrick to look forward to? Why had she allowed that small sliver of jealousy to shaft through her?

Angel plonked herself on the chair by the fireside instead of next to him on the sofa. She picked up her coffee-cup and sipped her coffee.

He zapped the TV off and the silence was deafening. He was the first to speak. 'Also, I wanted to take the call in private because I'm advising her on a personal matter.'

'Yes, an investment matter, I believe.' Angel couldn't resist stabbing back and knew immediately that she was a fool to herself.

He looked very slightly annoyed. 'So as well as eavesdropping in hotel restaurants you eavesdrop on phone calls too?'

Angel opted to stare into the fire rather than at him. 'Yes, I heard you talking of business matters in the restaurant and, because you're in investments, I just presumed that if you were dishing out advice just now it wouldn't be advice about what diet to try!'

Hugo laughed softly. 'Are you implying that Caroline would benefit from a diet?'

Angel flushed. She hadn't meant to sound catty but it must have sounded that way to him.

'No, it was just a figure of speech. Something that just came out. I didn't mean anything by it.'

'Pity,' he said in a low voice. 'It would be interesting to hear you say something vindictive about her.'

Angel shrugged. 'Sorry to disappoint you but I am *not* jealous.'

'Just a little curious,' he mocked. His eyes gleamed darkly, and once again she was flushed with the thought that Claudia had fallen so easily for him. Probably Caroline too and all the others. She wasn't one of the others, though, she thought resolutely.

'Not even that,' she uttered in a couldn't-care-less tone.

'So you are immune to my charms, are you? Probably why you're sitting over there and I'm all alone and lost on this sea of a sofa.'

'Lost on this sea of a sofa,' she repeated sarcastically but with softness in her voice. She smiled. 'That's nearly as bad as ''Come one step closer and I'll blast you to hell and back''.'

He smiled. 'You sound like my editor. Did you manage to read any more of my book?'

She nodded and curled her feet under her. 'Yes, I concentrated hard.' She had, though it had been hard to switch him off from her conscience. And she knew it would be hard to switch him off from her life when she left here. Oh, God, what was happening to her? Why wasn't Patrick here with her instead of this charismatic man she should be hating with her heart and her soul?

'Come to bed with me,' he said softly and unexpectedly.

A spark from the fire spat and fizzed and Angel felt it as if a shard of flame had entered her heart. She looked at him and held his eyes, and it was quite easy to do that because she was so stunned by the suggestion. Stunned and so very excited. Her pulses tipped crazily and a refusal didn't come to her lips straight away. In a split-second she considered it, fast-forwarded her emotions and her body into his very being. She could almost feel him touching her, running his hands sensuously over her body. She knew what his kisses were like but his penetration of her was but a heated fantasy. But she knew it would come up to expectations, and more.

'No,' she said at last, and he didn't look surprised or hurt or disappointed. She didn't doubt for a minute that he *did* want her and she didn't think that he was teasing her. He wanted her, not necessarily now, but some time soon. Those blatant words were the prelude to what was to come, what he thought was inevitable. By making his needs obvious it cut out the middleman of foreplay. Angel knew it and accepted it, and yet was still excited by the frankness of him.

'I won't ask you again, Angel. I did say the rest was up to you.'

She nodded slightly. 'It's not in my nature to take the initiative in that way,' she told him truthfully. 'I'm not Angel pure, Angel white, but it doesn't mean I could do what you want just like that.'

'You need time to think about it?' He frowned as if he didn't like the idea of that one bit.

She shook her head and lowered her eyes. 'Not even that.' She gave a small smile and looked up at him then. 'What did you expect when you asked me to go to bed with you? Did you really think I would say yes?'

He smiled. 'Yes, I did, and I can say that because I know you won't be offended by it. It isn't offensive to think of such a thing after we've only known each other such a short time, because some things are meant to be.'

Angel said quietly, 'Don't spoil it by getting all mystic about it.'

He leaned forward and looked at her seriously. 'Mysticism doesn't come into it. I want to go to bed with you and you want to go to bed with me. It's very straightforward, but what isn't straightforward is what you *think* you can make of it all.'

'I'm not looking for a commitment from you,' she protested. 'It's not that! Heavens, I have a commitment to Patrick. I'm sure going to bed with you would be very nice, but...'

'But what? You want more than nice?'

She stared at him obliquely. He didn't know what he had just said. Yes, she wanted more than nice. Patrick was nice, their relationship was nice. She didn't want nice, she wanted what he was offering, what this Hugo Drake-Latimer had so blatantly asked of her—damned, wretched excitement.

'I'm going to bed,' she told him, leaping to her feet. 'Alone and, yes, it is a cop-out and I'm not afraid to admit it.'

'What are you afraid of, then?' He reached forward and took her hand and the touch was confirmation of that fear.

'I'm afraid for my sanity,' she told him quietly. 'Because so far you've been very right about me and I'm acting out of character. If I went to bed with you I could easily lose my mind completely.'

He nodded sagely and that seemed to confirm that he thought insanity a possibility for her, and sooner rather than later. His mouth on the back of her hand was temptation at its most evil. Angel bit her lip and fought the urge to clench her fingers around his and so give him the incentive to go on. A simple kiss on the back of the hand? What hope would there be for her heart and her body *and* her sanity if she allowed his sensuality somewhere more intimate than her hand and her mouth?

CHAPTER FIVE

'I DIDN'T really expect you to rise at the crack of dawn to cook my breakfast,' Hugo said as he came into the kitchen the next morning.

'I know you didn't. The sun woke me up and I guessed you'd want to be up early. Writers do, don't they, rise early when the inspiration is at its most active?'

'Do they?' he muttered, inspecting the scrambled eggs which were fluffing in the microwave.

Angel glanced out of the window as she slid bread into the toaster. The sun was still shining and it looked as if it might be warm outside, and warmth and sunshine meant evaporation. Could a whole lake evaporate enough in a couple of hours to give her her freedom? The freedom she wasn't sure she wanted.

'If this weather holds you could be out of here tomorrow.'

His voice was light but Angel saw it as something much deeper. She felt he was testing her to see her reactions to the thought of leaving.

'What about today?' She poured hot water into the teapot and waited for *his* reaction.

'I don't want you to go today.'

Angel allowed a small thrill to ripple through her.

'Any reason?' she tempted.

'Not one that you don't know of already.'

She nodded and went to the microwave for the eggs. 'It will give you another night to try and get me into your bed.'

She thought he might be annoyed by that but he wasn't. 'People make love in the daytime too. Do you, with Patrick?'

'Do what with Patrick—make love in the daytime?' She couldn't remember a time they ever had. She dished up the breakfast and sat down at the table across from him. He'd said nothing and she poured the tea and narrowed her eyes at him.

'Why do you keep needling me about Patrick?'

He looked at her directly. 'I like you and don't want you to make a mistake in your life.'

So now he only liked her. Yesterday he thought he might be falling in love with her but of course that was part of his seduction ploy. She wondered how he would react if she told him she hadn't a fortune to her name. Would he be quite so attentive?

'I like you too,' she admitted, and it was some admission—the truth, though her reasoning screamed it shouldn't be, 'but I don't keep goading you about Caroline.'

'You did last night.'

'Yes, I suppose I did,' she murmured, and forked her eggs.

'So, we like each other. It's a good start.'

'The start of what?'

He shrugged. 'Whatever you have in mind.'

'I've nothing in mind.'

'But you had when you followed me here.'

He delivered that with a coolness that amazed Angel. It was still troubling him, her excuse for being here. He hadn't ever believed that she had simply got lost.

'I told you I didn't follow you, and anyway that's history now. You've survived and there were no silver blades flashing in the night.'

'Precious little else either,' he uttered morosely.

Angel smiled. 'Whatever did you expect?'

'I didn't expect anything when I hauled you out of your car that night, but things change. Now I want you. I desire you. I think you want what I want——'

'A change from our regular partners?' Angel suggested with a shake of her head. 'You disappoint me.'

'Don't be disappointed, because that wasn't what I meant at all.'

She reached for some toast and so did he and their hands touched. Angel sprang back from him as if she had been stung. He noticed.

'You see. It's there—the chemistry.'

Bravely Angel remarked, 'I don't deny its existence but it isn't everything.'

'You're right, it isn't. After another couple of days here, when we get to know each other better, we might find that we don't even fancy each other any more.'

Angel said nothing. She couldn't deny it because it would be a give-away. But she could deny in her own heart that her feelings were good. She shouldn't be liking him, she shouldn't even be considering the things she was when he looked at her a certain way. She *should* keep reminding herself of what he had done to Claudia's heart and her bank balance. And she was trying but failing. She now understood how easy it was to become a gangster's moll. A certain type of woman fell for mean crooks. Was she one of that certain type of woman?

'Why do you think women fall for rogues?' she asked him after a moment's thought on the subject. Because he wrote about crime and criminals he surely wouldn't think the question untoward?

'Lovable rogues, like men who tamper with women's affections for the hell of it, or the hardened criminal who robs banks?'

'The hardened criminal.'

'Why the interest? Do you know one?'

He was studying her intently when she looked up from her plate to meet his eyes. They were mesmeric eyes, holding and penetrating at the same time. But they weren't suspicious eyes and that was no consolation to Angel. He was probably far cleverer than the average con man and he probably didn't think he'd done any wrong in swindling beautiful women anyway.

'No,' she said. 'I don't mix in criminal circles—at least, I don't think I do, but I suppose these days you don't know who you're rubbing shoulders with.'

It was a meaningful remark and she watched his face for a give-away reaction, maybe a tightening of a facial muscle, a flicker of the eyes. Nothing. Mr Cool.

'Your book made me think of it,' she went on. 'I know it's fiction but I'm sure you base some of it on fact—certainly the interaction between characters, the women and their menfolk. So why are these women attracted to the criminal element?'

'Several reasons, but I suspect the main reason is that a woman in love always thinks she'll be the one to change him.'

'So it isn't the criminal element she falls for, she just hopes that he's so crazy about her he'll change his life of crime for her.'

She thought she understood that. Yes, she did understand it. She could already be thinking about making *him* see the error of his ways. So did that mean she was falling in love with him and hoping he was falling in love with her? Wow, what a thought.

'On the other hand,' he went on, and now he leaned forward to stress his point, 'there are certain women who get a definite buzz out of being associated with a man who takes such risks in his life.'

Ah, was that something else to consider—that he did what he did because he enjoyed the risk, and did she find him so fascinating because she knew him to be a thief? No, that wasn't the attraction. In fact it was the one thing holding her off from him. She liked everything else about him but what he had done to Claudia and what he was about to do to Caroline. In a way she was glad of that, because Patrick was very much on her conscience. Instead of romanticising about Hugo Drake-Latimer she should be getting her relationship with Patrick into perspective. He was the real world.

'You've gone very quiet,' he prompted after a long silence between them. He reached for the teapot and

Angel slid it towards him. 'Were you thinking of Patrick just then?'

Her heart thudded at that. He really was very perceptive.

'Yes, I was actually,' she admitted. What would be the point in denying it?

'Is he a criminal?'

Angel smiled. 'No, of course not. He's far too respectable to consider breaking the law.'

'So I'm right, you are finding him boring and that's why you're attracted to me.'

She couldn't even be mad at his arrogance because the smile that went with such a chauvinistic remark was so warm and endearing.

'What are you trying to say—that you harbour criminal tendencies?' It was a daring question and she wondered at her own nerve in asking it, but she shouldn't wonder really. Something had happened to Angel Weston lately and she was quite enjoying it, so why question it?

'I couldn't break the law if I tried,' he told her quietly. 'I don't have it in me, and certainly my life-style doesn't necessitate my turning to crime to support myself.'

Angel looked at him long and hard. In any other circumstances she wouldn't even question that statement. She would believe it, unfailingly. But Claudia clawed her way into her reasoning, and a Hugo Drake-Latimer had cheated her and broken her heart and just because he didn't need the money it didn't mean he was incapable of doing it. Cheating women could be his work experience and give him an added thrill in life to boot. Suddenly she didn't want to think of her cousin any more. Surely she was capable of making a decision about the man on her own findings? He had flirted with her—well, a little more than that—but not once had he mentioned investments to her, and surely the two went together?

But perhaps they didn't. Perhaps his only motive for flirting with her was because he actually liked her *and* desired her.

He started to clear the table and Angel didn't want to let him go. 'But... but you write about crime, so it must fascinate you, so there must be something like that in you,' she persisted.

He laughed and slid a pile of dishes on to the top of the dishwasher ready to be loaded. 'Yes, crime fascinates me as it fascinates most people, and that's why my sort of books sell so well and every other programme on TV is crime-orientated. We as human beings thrill to it. We don't all go out and commit crimes, though. We need fantasy in our lives.'

He looked down at her. 'And what is your fantasy, your escapism?'

Angel held his eyes for a second and then looked away. 'I haven't one,' she said quietly. She got up and started to clear away the plates he had left, but he stopped her. His hand came out and stilled hers and she left the plates where they were. Gently he pulled her towards him.

'You must have a fantasy,' he told her. 'It's a safety-valve, something you have that you have created for yourself and no one can spoil. You can fall back on it when things are bloody.'

She shook her head and tried to draw back from him but it was a feeble attempt. She wanted to be in his arms; she wanted him to kiss her again. Was that her fantasy?

'If I had a fantasy I wouldn't tell you anyway. It wouldn't be a fantasy if I did. It wouldn't be mine any more.'

'Fantasies can be shared and fulfilled.' The tone of his voice made it sound like an invitation.

'And then you'd have to move on to the next fantasy because that's the point of fantasies: they're something unobtainable.'

'But sometimes you get the chance to live them and when you do you take that chance because it might never happen again.'

Angel gazed up at him and smiled ruefully. 'Are you trying to tell me something?'

'I'm trying to tempt you,' he breathed softly. 'At the moment you are my fantasy and I want it fulfilled, in every possible way.'

'Just because I'm here?' she breathed tremulously.

His hand came up and cupped her face and the touch was tender and so very tempting that she wanted to melt into his arms. But she couldn't. It was as simple as that. She just couldn't.

'Yes, because you're here. You came into my life unexpectedly and that must be some sort of kismet.'

Love by chance, Angel thought. But it wasn't love for him. He'd said it all: take that chance because it might never happen again. He didn't see this relationship progressing further than these few days stranded on Summer Island.

And she had no right to expect or even consider anything more. He had his Caroline and she had her Patrick . . .

His mouth was suddenly on hers and the kiss spun Caroline and Patrick out of her mind. She knew then the thrill of danger and she knew and understood something she had never thought she would ever experience. Wanting someone with such a deep desire that it shook your very roots. Only days ago she had been wondering about desire and passion and thinking she hadn't got it in her, but she had. This man kissing her so stunningly now was offering her the gateway to heaven, a heaven she hadn't thought existed for her.

His hands crawled sensuously around her back, moulding her body into his till they were one. He was hard against her and her blood coursed hotly around her body, signalling the awakening of her senses.

Excitement and passion roared around her till she almost lost her breath with the intensity of the feeling. He held her so firmly and was so much in control that she was weak and very nearly senseless under the urgency of his lips on hers.

Her whole body seemed to swell under the onslaught of his need and her heart surged with the thrill of knowing she could excite him so. And then the ultimate of sensations rattled her so badly that she let out a ragged gasp. His hand had eased up under her sweater, and she was so drugged with sensation that she hadn't even been aware of it. Now the soft caress of his fingers across her breast was a fiery awakening.

Her nipples swelled chaotically under the pressure and then his mouth drew back from hers.

Her eyes were glazed as she stared up at him. He looked down at her and there was an enigmatic smile on his lips. He kept up the pulsing pressure on her breast and nipple, his thumb stroking backwards and forwards tantalisingly.

She wanted more, more than she had ever wanted anything in her life. She wanted Hugo to make love to her, to be inside her. She wanted it all with him . . . and he knew.

'Am I your fantasy at the moment?' he whispered as he gazed down at her, knowing, knowing. 'Do you want me inside you? Do you want me to love you completely and as no other man has ever loved you before?'

Her throat had seized up completely. He knew so much, he sensed so much and she knew nothing. Nothing was a consideration now. Not his cheating ways nor his cheating heart could touch her now. Love by chance—it had hit her. She accepted it but didn't understand it.

She rested her hands on the crook of his arms. Those hands had rampaged through his hair as he had kissed her. Only now could she register that she had done that. What else had she done under the spell-binding mist of sensuality he had spun around her? Had she touched him as he had so intimately touched her?

He took one of her hands and clasped it to his chest. She felt the thud of his heart under her palm. It beat out his desire and his eyes showed that desire and she felt that desire hard against her groin. She closed her eyes with a peculiar kind of suffering. Desire was a form of suffering when it was so impossible.

'Let go, Angel,' he murmured softly. 'Think of nothing but the moment.'

Her voice came at last. 'I am thinking of the moment,' she admitted in a very weak whisper. 'But the moment will pass and this ... this feeling will pass——'

'I think not,' he said gravely, and he shifted her hand and moved it down and she felt a hot flush of colour rise to her face and engulf her.

'You're blushing.'

'I'm embarrassed,' she croaked as she tried to wriggle her fingers out of his and away from that terrible temptation he was pressing her hand against.

'You shouldn't be embarrassed; you should be very proud of what you can do to me.'

'And pride comes before a fall,' she uttered, and with all her strength she pulled away from him.

He didn't force her back but simply let his hands run down her arms to her wrists, and then she felt his fingers coil around her own.

'I hope it rains forever,' he said softly.

'Or until I give in,' she said strongly. The weakness he had pressured her into was fading.

He smiled thinly. 'I don't think you will, but don't expect any admiration from me for your iron reserve not to be used.'

She raised an eyebrow. 'Is that what you think— that I'm afraid to let go for fear of being used?'

He shrugged slightly, his broad shoulders such a temptation to grasp hold of. 'It's usually the reason, isn't it?'

'I wouldn't know. I've never been confronted with this situation before.'

He nodded. 'So you are Angel pure.'

Angel shook her head. 'I meant that I've never been propositioned quite so early in a relationship and I'm not suggesting we have one—a relationship—but we certainly have a situation here.'

'A curious one too.'

Yes, it was a curious situation, isolated as they were away from the world, hardly knowing each other and yet wanting each other this way. Sexual chemistry. It was the first time she had come up against it. It hadn't been that way with Patrick. Theirs was a love formed on a friendship and a mutual respect for each other except that now, because of this man before her, it had floundered badly. How could she love Patrick when another man had impinged so acutely on her psyche?

'A damaging one,' Angel corrected, and Hugo's eyes narrowed slightly.

'How can it be damaging?'

His voice was quite cold and his normal good humour wasn't very apparent. She supposed he was offended by the suggestion that he could do harm to anyone. His annoyance stirred her own and all she knew about him, all she had forgotten when his passion had tempted her so, flushed to the surface once again.

'You can't see it, can you? You can't see that what you're trying to do with me *is* damaging. I have someone in my life, someone I care about, but you seem hell-bent on changing my mind about him.' She shrugged and drew her hands out of his. 'And what for? To prove that you can bed me better than he can?'

His eyes suddenly flared and a chord of anger tightened at his throat. He didn't speak, though; not one word came from his tight lips. He gave her one last searching look and then he turned away from her. She heard him cross the hallway and his study door close softly but firmly after him.

Angel let out one long, anguished cry of protest; she wasn't sure whom it was aimed at. It was just a release to let out all her hot air. But she was right. His assault on her was damaging, though not to him— he had nothing to lose but his writing time while they made love. She doubted Caroline was a consideration. But she had her heart to consider, and Patrick. It wasn't a case of her conscience troubling her. She hadn't done anything wrong, but if fantasies counted her conscience would be rattling.

But damn him, Hugo Drake-Latimer. With very little effort he had changed her world. How could she go back to Patrick with the same affection now? She smiled ruefully. Affection, that was what she felt for Patrick, and Hugo with his outspokenness and his damned sexuality had made her realise that. But why should she suddenly know that life with Patrick would be predictable and passionless? Because Hugo had put temptation in her way and spoiled everything she had felt for Patrick.

In a way she despised him for that, in another she was grateful. He had put her future on the line. She couldn't marry Patrick now or even carry on the relationship. It was over.

'And you are not a consideration,' Angel breathed under her breath as she cleared up the kitchen. 'You are just a scapegoat for my conscience. Thanks for nothing!'

By late afternoon the sunshine had been blazing for hours. Angel thought she ought to check her car, and while she was outside she'd check to see if the causeway had appeared out of nowhere.

She found her car keys on the hall table and went outside. The car started first time, which surprised her considering the damp conditions. She let the car engine tick over while she went across the garden to look for the causeway.

Her hand went to her heart as she saw what she had negotiated. The causeway was just visible through the murky water of the lake, but what lay on either side of it was impossible to judge. It could be only inches of water or feet. She could so easily have gone off the edge. She shuddered, and suddenly she felt comforting hands on her shoulders. His, of course.

'Doesn't look half so menacing in the daylight, does it?' he said in her ear.

'Thank God I didn't see it at night. I'd have gone right over the edge for sure. Sheer terror would have panicked me off the road.'

'It's really quite wide, much wider than you imagine, and the edges are gently banked, so if you had gone off no harm would have come to you. You might have got your feet wet, or even your ankles, but that's all.'

'You should have told me that when I arrived.'

'Then you wouldn't have stayed.'

She was slightly thrilled to find he had wanted her to stay from the start, but the feeling didn't last as he added, 'And I'd have never found out why you followed me.'

'And you still haven't,' she told him, knowing she was running the risk of him opening up the inquisition again, but she felt they had come so far that now it had quietened to more of a joke than anything.

'Ah, but I have. You were looking for excitement.'

'Ah, yes, I remember.' She walked away from him and went to switch off her ignition before she ran out of petrol and was forced to spend the rest of her life here. 'Tell me, why did you buy this place?' she asked as he came up beside her. He leaned back on her bonnet and she went on, 'It's not the usual run-of-the-mill holiday cottage.'

He gazed lovingly at his grey stone cottage. 'Oh, I don't know. It looks pretty traditional to me.'

She leaned back on the bonnet next to him. 'Not the situation, though. That's distinctly non-traditional. I mean, you could come here for the weekend and it rains and you end up being forced to stay for weeks.'

'Exactly.' He was squinting up at the roof now and Angel followed his gaze. 'I like the unpredictable.'

She supposed he must. The money market, crime, both very unpredictable. He liked taking risks in his life, he enjoyed living out his fantasies and his scams, in life and in his books.

'It's why I like you,' he added. 'You did a crazy thing following me here. You're unpredictable too.'

She never had been before. But before what? Before that strange whim had taken her over? She shivered slightly at the thought of what she had done and how it had turned out. Hugo had changed her life and all by chance.

'What are you looking at?'

Hugo stepped forward and shielded his eyes as he gazed up more intently now. 'That rain must have had some power behind it. I think I've got a few roof-tiles loose.'

Angel smiled wickedly. 'A few screws loose too, if you ask me.'

He turned to her but said nothing about her jokey insult. He grinned. 'How are you at holding ladders?'

Her eyes widened and flashed from his wide smile to the offending roof. 'You're not thinking of going up there and fixing them yourself?' she asked in amazement.

He obviously was. She watched in horror as he dragged an extending ladder from the garage. Angel's heart began to pound as he propped it up against the side of the stone cottage.

'Just stand at the bottom and break my fall if I slip.' He was laughing but Angel didn't find it amusing. He could kill himself up there.

'You talk about me being crazy,' she grumbled as she took up her position at the foot of the ladder while he scaled it as a cat-burglar might. Did he do that too—burgle?

She gazed up at him as he calmly stepped off the ladder and scrambled on to the gently sloping roof. She was far from calm, though. Her heart was wedged firmly in her throat and her nerves shook so badly she could almost hear them rattling. Her fears were confirmed then and somehow it wasn't a surprise, maybe because she was getting used to whimsy and fate and kismet. She *was* in love. Here and now, and this fear she felt was love because the thought of him slipping and falling to the ground in a fatal tragedy was a fantasy so heart-rippingly scary that she knew love was behind it.

'Oh, my God,' she whispered to herself as her breathing quickened. 'This couldn't have happened.' But it had, and her stomach rolled with the realisation and then she couldn't bear it any longer.

'Hugo!' she called out.

He grunted above her.

Angel felt herself slipping. 'Hugo, please,' she wailed. 'Get down . . . please get down . . .'

'I won't be a minute.'

It will be too late, she mouthed as her mouth went numb and the rolling of her insides was only superseded by the rolling of her head. She leaned back against the ladder and as the whirling blackness surrounded her she slid down the lower rungs and fainted in a heap on the wet grass at the base of the ladder.

* * *

'What happened?' she heard him murmur through space.

'What happened?' she repeated faintly. Her eyes felt heavy but at least the nausea had gone and her head had stopped spinning and her breathing wasn't so harsh and ragged. She focused on his face hovering so worriedly above her. He cares too, she thought, but it was such a fleeting thought that it didn't quite register and stick.

'You fainted, but why I can't imagine. You're not pregnant, are you?'

'I'm not pregnant,' she told him, and struggled to sit up.

'Stay,' he ordered, and held a glass of water to her lips. 'So what happened?'

'Vertigo,' she uttered weakly, and sank back against the cushions after sipping some water. She was on the sofa and she could only have got there if he had carried her.

He smiled. 'Good try,' he offered lightly. 'But not good enough. It was me on the roof, not you.'

'Vertigo by proxy. I had it for you.'

'Impossible. Come on, lovely, be honest and make my day.'

A knowing grin refused to budge from the corners of his mouth. He knows, she thought miserably. Knowing she loved him was one thing, *him* knowing she loved him was something else.

'And wipe that grin from your face,' she ordered, not very strongly. 'Fainting isn't funny. Imagine if it had been me on that roof instead of you.'

'But it wasn't, and it was because it was me that I find your fainting so interesting.'

She tried to get up then but he wouldn't let her. Gently he pushed her back on to the cushions. 'You panicked, didn't you?'

'Don't be absurd!'

'It's true. You panicked for me, your breath quickened, you hyperventilated and went out like a light. All because you're so crazy about me that the thought of me slipping was unbearable for you.'

Oh, he was so damned smart! Angel narrowed her eyes at him. 'When I was nine years old I was watching an old film on TV. King Kong was wavering on the top of the Empire State Building. I was so terrified he'd fall, I passed out then. My mother nearly fainted with shock too. She forbade me to watch horror movies after that, which I thought was a bit unfair. The movie didn't scare me. I just care about creatures, even big, hairy ones like Kong.'

'So it was nothing personal?' he queried, with laughter in his tone.

'Absolutely not. Satisfied?' She glowered at him.

'You know the only satisfaction I want,' he teased in a low voice.

'Yes.' She sighed wearily, and went to get up. 'Unfortunately I do.'

'Stay where you are,' he told her firmly but kindly. 'I'll fix dinner.' He switched on the television for her. 'Watch the news for me and report, and try not to faint over the weather forecast.'

She poked her tongue out at the closed door.

Later they ate supper on their laps and watched a game show, and then Angel made coffee and Hugo played the piano.

She sat curled up on the sofa sipping brandy and coffee and listened as he played an Errol Garner favourite. Then he sat with her and they talked quietly for a long time. She told him about her parents working and living in Singapore and he told her about his sister, Laura, who was a dancer in a West End musical, and how his own parents thoroughly disapproved but nevertheless saw the show at least twice a week when they were in town.

Later when Angel was undressing for bed she wondered what had happened. He hadn't made a pass at her all evening. She liked to think it was because he had been so concerned for her after that silly panic attack, but of course when you were in love gremlins were always at your reasoning, poking their interfering little fingers in where they weren't wanted. It was more than likely that now he believed she wasn't interested in him. Perhaps the comparison with King Kong had got to him. Perhaps he had simply grown bored with her.

Whatever, she was going to leave in the morning. Unless, of course, the heavens opened again tonight. She had a feeling they wouldn't, and she had a feeling that sleep wouldn't come easily, and she was right about both.

CHAPTER SIX

'YOU'LL be leaving this morning, then?'

He'd been up for hours. She'd heard him showering, then he had gone downstairs and there was silence. She'd suspected that he was working but hadn't known for sure as she'd lain curled up in her bed, reluctant to get up and face a bright, sunny day. Eventually she had got up, though, and stared out of the window. It wasn't just a bright, sunny day, it was a glorious one, a day for a picnic by the lake, a lazy boat ride through the still waters and strolling hand in hand through a fragrant, damp pine forest. All fantasy.

She faced him in the kitchen, dressed in what she'd come in—the black dress and the shabby Aran cardigan.

'Yes, I must,' she said quietly. 'I...I've put Laura's clothes, the ones I've worn, in a pile on the foot of the bed. Thank her for me.'

'Why must you go?' he asked. The kettle was sizzling behind him and he turned to switch it off, and Angel briefly flicked shut her eyes in pain.

She didn't want to go but to stay would be quite ridiculous.

He faced her once again and she couldn't meet his eyes. She didn't *want* to meet his eyes in case she floundered.

'I have to go, you know I must. The weather is clear and if it rains again——'

'You'll have to stay and you really don't want to, do you?'

He sounded quite regretful, and she supposed that must be because she wasn't a conquest and it probably mattered to his ego.

'I must go,' she murmured. 'I have to get back to work and . . .' There really wasn't anything more she could say.

'You've had no breakfast.'

She shrugged. 'I'll have it at the hotel.'

'And then what will you do?'

She shrugged. 'Pack and leave the hotel and drive home.'

'And where is home?'

He didn't even know where she lived and he wouldn't either, because that would give the game away. He'd probably taken Claudia home on numerous occasions. Claudia should be back from Greece now and the thought of facing her wasn't a pleasant one. She couldn't tell her who she had been with these past days, because nothing fruitful had come out of her time spent with Hugo Drake-Latimer. At the beginning of this fiasco she had nurtured ideas of exposing him and perhaps getting Claudia's money back, but that had all fallen by the wayside as she had fallen—yes, it was no good denying it—she had fallen in love with him. And because she had fallen in love she knew she didn't want to go on believing that he was some sort of felon any more. Claudia could have made a mistake after all: money markets were tricky and the share plunge could have been genuine. But... but she knew nothing for sure so it was better blocked out from her mind.

'And where is home, Angel?' Hugo persisted, shaking her out of her thoughts.

'Manchester,' she told him vaguely.

'Manchester is a big place.'

'Yes,' she agreed. 'Very big.' She squared her shoulders and looked him bravely in the eye. 'Can I have my car keys?'

He must have them because they weren't in the car or on the hall table. Yesterday she had left them in the car, before she had fainted.

He shrugged. 'I haven't got them ... Just a minute, yes, I have, upstairs in my jeans pocket.' He smiled slightly. 'While I'm getting them you might as well make some tea or coffee——'

'No,' Angel interjected on a sigh. She just wanted to go, and now, before it got worse.

'OK, I won't be a minute.'

He left her standing in the kitchen and she thought it must only take a minute for him to run up and get her keys from his bedroom, but he seemed to be taking forever. Her eyes settled on his latest book he had lent her. She'd brought it down from her bedroom and placed it on the kitchen table. She would put it back in his study in case he told her to keep it. She couldn't bear it if he did. She wanted no reminders.

He had been working while she'd lain in bed. The fire in his study hadn't been lit but his computer was on. She stepped towards it and took a sharp intake of breath when she read what was on the screen. 'Angel pure, Angel bright . . .'

Suddenly the screen went blank as his hand snaked past her to switch it off. Angel turned to him and the look in his dark eyes had her heart leaping like a week-old spring lamb.

'So now you know,' he said, so softly that she only just heard it.

'Kn-know what?' she stuttered weakly, her skin tingling with excitement. He must have been thinking about her while he was working and . . . and . . .

'That I can't get you out of my mind,' he admitted hoarsely. He lifted a hand to smooth it down the side of her face, and the softness of his touch brought a flush of hot colour to her cheeks. 'I don't want you to go,' he went on, his tone so soft and persuasive that she almost fell into his arms. 'I want you to stay——'

'No,' she cried, so forcefully that she surprised herself. She pulled back from him and his hand dropped to his side.

'I tried to work this morning but it was impossible,' he went on, completely ignoring her withdrawal from him. His eyes were so dark and inviting, inviting her to let go of her last ounce of reserve. 'You make it impossible for me to concentrate. I want to possess you and I can't think of anything else but taking you to my bed and making love to you.'

Angel could hardly breathe. When he talked like this it unnerved her. She wanted him too, and because he was so unlike anyone she had met before. Because he was open and frank about his needs and she found him so exciting. Patrick... No, Patrick wasn't an issue here. Patrick didn't own her, but she felt that if this man before her had his way she would be solely possessed, solely owned and taken over. What of her life beyond him? Would there be one? How easily she could understand Claudia now.

She drew fiercely on her bottom lip as he moved in on her again. One kiss and the decision would be made, to love him or not...

'There are worse decisions to make in life, Angel pure,' he murmured, so close to her mouth that she could almost taste him.

She couldn't think of one. This was surely the worst decision she had ever been faced with. Temptation: it was such an emotive word. She wanted to give in to it. She had never been exposed to it before, her life had never thrown it at her before... and... and she hadn't the strength of will to toss it back and run from here.

'Angel,' he murmured.

It was neither a plea nor acceptance, just a terrible temptation, and as his lips found hers she felt the ground shift from under her and she knew it would never right itself again.

Their lips touched, their tongues touched, softly, softly. So sensuously, so beautifully. He slid his hands around her waist and oh, so tenderly drew her to him. And she was lost, her head and heart spinning, her whole being dizzy with need for him.

They were in his bedroom, his bright, sunny bedroom. He had taken her hand and led her here and she had come, hardly aware that she was moving.

But now the brightness brought her up with a start. And he knew and he was oh, so astute. He smiled knowingly and moved away from her to the curtains at the windows. With a swish they cut out the glare of the sun, just leaving enough to cast a soft light into the room.

Then he turned to her and held out his hands and she knew that she had to make the decision now. She still had space enough to get out of it, her mind told her feebly, but her heart made the choice for her. He looked so wonderfully exciting standing waiting for her expectantly. So tall and impressively built, so dramatic in close-fitting jeans and black cashmere sweater. His jet hair was too long, excitingly too long, curling around the collar of the black silk shirt he wore under his sweater.

She longed to touch the silk of that shirt, to feel his warmth and strength beneath it. She wanted all of him.

He said her name again, and the desire in the depth of his voice had deepened and it thrilled her.

She found her voice and uttered his name helplessly, but couldn't make those few steps towards him.

'Come to me, Angel,' he murmured. 'It isn't so very hard to do, is it?'

She felt small and foolish and yet her heart beat wildly inside her. Did he know what he was doing to her? Making her take the initiative. Those few steps were submission, and somehow she felt that if she took them her life would never be the same again. And suddenly she knew that she didn't want her life to be the same again. It couldn't ever be the same again anyway. She loved him and she had never loved before, not like this, with the thrill and heart-leaping compulsion that was tipping her insides crazily. He had brought life to her life.

She took those few steps towards him and slowly she brought her small hands up to meet his. He took them and entwined his fingers around hers and it was a bond that couldn't be broken.

Her lips were already parted when he kissed her, her heart was already his, her desire was as powerful as his, and she wasn't afraid any more. He let go of her hands to wrap his own around her body and the tremor that ran through her couldn't be concealed.

'I hope that's passion and not fear,' he murmured in her hair. 'You're not afraid, are you?'

'No, not afraid,' she whispered, and to show she wasn't she lifted her arms and slid them around his neck and buried her face in his neck. She thought it was a very girlish thing to do, not sophisticated or worldly. Would he think she was naïve? Would he be disappointed in her?

He drew back from her and looked down into her eyes. 'You know, you're like no other woman I've ever met.'

She *was* unworldly. She *would* be a disappointment to him. But no. This wasn't Patrick with his unintentional put-downs; this was a man who knew how to treat a woman, this was a man who truly wanted to make love to her, on her terms, not his. He'd been patient and caring and he was funny and so very different and she wouldn't be a disappointment because a man like him wouldn't allow it.

Angel smiled, lifted her lips to his and bravely slid her hands under his sweater, and the strength of his body beneath the silk of his shirt was all she expected it to be. Her touch seemed to force a new power to his mouth and his kisses grew more heated.

He eased her cardigan from her shoulders; it fell to the floor and she lifted her head to look at him, bewildered because she didn't know what to expect next from him.

'I . . . I can manage the rest,' she uttered weakly.

A half-smile crossed his lips. 'And spoil my fun.'

She stiffened at that. Was this just fun to him?

He grasped her tighter in case she thought of running. 'No, sweet Angel, it isn't what you think. I want to undress you, every inch of you, because you will enjoy it as much as I will.'

He proved it by sensuously unzipping her dress and slowly, slowly peeling it down till her breasts were exposed for him to see and touch and kiss. Her head arched back as his lips grazed across the peaks of her breasts, his tongue teasing and circling her nipples till the desire was almost a pain crying for release. The dress crumpled to the floor and she stood naked but for her tiny briefs, dazed and slightly trembling with this new sensation of being so exposed to him. His hands slid the silk from her hips and his mouth closed heatedly over hers to stem the small cry she couldn't help forming in her throat. She ached for him and yet still she hadn't felt his nakedness close to her, and she knew that when she did the feeling would be overwhelming.

She was naked and unashamed and this exhilarating sense of freedom gave her the confidence to move her hands up under his sweater to unbutton his shirt beneath. He stepped back and scooped his sweater off and out of her way and then with a ragged gasp of desire he lifted her up into his arms and laid her on the bed. She reached for him but he stood by the side of the bed gazing down at her, hungrily running his eyes over her body till she burned under his gaze. He didn't even have to touch her and she was fired with a passion that must surely show.

She watched him, her eyes wide, as he unzipped his jeans, kicked out of them then shrugged off his shirt. He stood there, so hard and proud, his body so powerful that for a second she thought she might fail him at the last moment. She closed her eyes as he came to her on the bed, suddenly shy, but he gathered her hard against him and all inhibitions left her. She clung to him as he powered kisses of desire across her mouth, her throat, across her breasts, a fiery path of kisses flowing across her skin till she arched beneath him, hardly able to bear the force of need that contracted every muscle in her body.

His kisses went on, down over her stomach and then ... She cried out then as his mouth rushed feverishly, searchingly... Oh, God, sweet, sweet, pulsing sensation had her clawing at his hair. Never before ... not like this. She struggled helplessly beneath him, twisting and writhing herself wantonly against him and suddenly his mouth came to hers and she tasted her own sweetness, and then with a shuddering gasp he was inside her. She cried out again.

Not a cry of pain or fear but one of pure sensation, one of joy and completeness, one of hunger for more and more.

She opened her eyes and he was above her, moving fiercely inside her, his body glistening and tensed in the soft light, the cords of muscle in his arms as he supported himself over her taut and rippling. He had her completely in his power as he moved. Hard strokes that thudded into her, delighting her more and more, urging her into a state of frenzy till she could hold on no longer. But she did hold on because to let go would be too soon. She wanted this heat and fire forever, she wanted him inside her forever but . . . it was impossible. She broke under him with an animal cry of release, a cry that had him shuddering his response as she clawed at his back. She felt him burst inside her as she was bursting with liquid fire and they clung together, gasping and trembling with the exertion of their fiery climax.

Their heartbeats filled the room; the heat from their bodies was intense. Angel lay half under him knowing that she loved him so deeply, so completely that it shut out the world. She didn't want to think of anything that didn't concern him. She wanted his life, not her own. She didn't want to be anywhere else but with him.

He stirred and rolled from her but she felt no rejection because immediately he gathered her into his arms and held her possessively against his body.

'I hope it rains forever,' he breathed.

He had said that once before, she remembered. She smiled against him and prayed for the same thing and refused to let the world encroach. Now was all that mattered. Tomorrow didn't exist.

She thought they must have slept. She wasn't sure. Time didn't exist. She felt his fingers smooth between her thighs and his mouth smooth across hers. She reached for him and touched him and later she tasted him. And later he loved her again and they stroked and explored each other and the feelings grew more fiery, more intense, till the obsession with each other's body was one that couldn't be broken. His libido was incredible, almost frightening in its intensity, and he aroused hers till she thought she wasn't herself but some new person who had emerged from the safe, protective chrysalis of Angel Weston.

Much, much later she drowsily rolled over and he wasn't there. She lay on her back and stared at the ceiling, straining her ears for the sound of him. She heard him downstairs, moving about in the kitchen.

Angel got up, aching with what her body had been through. A wonderful ache, though. She stood by the window and gingerly drew the curtain aside. The world was still there, bathed in spring sunshine. She could see across the lake now. The glint of a silver car on a distant road brought the world crashing in on her. With trembling fingers she let the curtain drop back across the window.

'I've made tea,' he said as he came back into the bedroom with a tray.

'Hugo,' she breathed from the bed where she sat hunched with a sheet wrapped tightly around her.

'Don't,' he said quickly. He was wearing a dark blue robe and as he put the tray down on the bedside table it gaped open, revealing his beautiful body. A deep shyness assailed her, for how well she knew that body now.

'You don't know what I was going to say,' she said in a low voice.

'I can imagine,' he said quietly as he sat on the edge of the bed and poured the tea. He'd made sandwiches too, and though she was ravenous she knew she couldn't eat. She hungered for words, not food.

'I suppose you can,' she started, 'because none of this is new to you.'

'You're new to me, Angel, so please don't spoil it all by analysing what we've done together.' He looked at her. 'That was what you wanted to do, wasn't it?'

Angel shrugged her narrow shoulders, took the tea he offered and drank it in silence. At last she said, 'Yes, I suppose so. I . . . I've never . . . never done such things.'

His eyes softened and he spoke quietly. 'You were not Angel pure, though.'

She clenched her fingers around the cup she held. 'I never said I was. Patrick and I——'

'I don't want to hear about Patrick,' he cut in, and she knew she had been wrong to bring his name into it. He put his cup down and reached for hers, taking it from her clenched hand. He leaned across the bed, his lips touched hers and she closed her eyes and wanted to be far away from him. He had power and he had sucked her into his world and changed her, and now she knew that she should never have allowed it.

'I expect you want to run now,' he said when he drew back from her. 'I understand that and I won't stop you.'

Oh, God, she *wanted* him to stop her. She wanted him to say something that would bond them together forever and it was possible, surely? He wasn't married, she wasn't married. She'd known before this had happened that Patrick wasn't a part of her life any more but . . . but Caroline . . . was she still very much a part of his life?

'Yes, I have to go,' she said strongly. Life goes on, she told herself, but it was a pitiful turn of phrase and she was glad she hadn't spoken it out loud.

It wasn't easy to get up and dress and act as if this sort of thing were commonplace to her, but she was strengthened by the thought that it was probably very commonplace to him. By the time she was ready to leave he was dressed too. She took furtive glances at him but his face was impassive, stony, in fact.

In silence they went downstairs; in silence they went outside.

'I'll call you,' was all he said as she tightened her seatbelt around her.

Angel didn't say a word. She couldn't because her throat was dry and tight. She tried not to think; she wanted to block it all out from her mind because thinking hurt. She reversed, drove out of his yard and on to the causeway and only looked in the rear-view mirror once.

He was standing as solid as a rock, hands plunged into his jeans pockets, watching her disappearing out of his sight. She felt then that he didn't want her to go but didn't know what to say to stop her. The feeling filled her with hope, but then it was all cruelly dashed as she reached the other side of the causeway and turned into the main road, for the first car she passed was driven by someone she knew.

Angel's eyes blurred with tears so fiercely that she could hardly see, but the pain was over in a second because it had to be. Clear-eyed and with a stony heart she drove on. There was only one place Caroline could be going—across a devious causeway to a devious little island to see a devious man, Hugo Drake-Latimer. No wonder Hugo had let her go so easily.

'I've changed. I'm not the person you think I am any more,' she told Patrick as they sat on a bench by the canal bank.

The first thing she had done on her return from the Lake District was to phone to see if he was home. He was, and she'd arranged to meet him where they sometimes shared a hurried lunch together, on the canal bank not far from the office.

Angel had convinced herself that Hugo wasn't the reason for letting Patrick down, though she knew in her heart that he was partly to blame. She'd had her doubts about the relationship with Patrick before she had allowed Hugo to change her life. It was the reason she had spurred off to the Lakes in the first place and this was the only reason she gave to Patrick: doubts about taking their relationship any further. She didn't want to be cruel by mentioning Hugo.

'I had time to think about us while we were apart and it wouldn't be fair to you to carry on.'

Patrick was silent but appeared to be taking it well. He was pale, but then he often was.

'I'm thinking of moving on,' she continued. 'I've thought of going down to London to broaden my career.' And she had given it serious thought. She'd never see Hugo Drake-Latimer again. He had used her and she had allowed herself to be used and she wanted to forget that he had ever brightened her life.

'Have you a position in mind?' Patrick asked, and Angel wondered if the question was born of self-preservation for his own hurt feelings.

'No, not yet.' She gave a slight shrug.

'Personally I think you're making a grave mistake, Angel, leaving everything that's familiar to you. You have a good steady career with Railton, security for the future, a pension scheme that's a credit to the company...'

Heavens! A pension scheme... She was only twenty-three! Where was talk of love and missing her if she went? Oh, dear Patrick, you ease my guilt, Angel mused to herself.

She stood up and Patrick stood up with her. 'I'm really sorry, Patrick,' Angel murmured genuinely.

He shrugged and smiled thinly. 'We would have made a good team, Angel. We would have had a golden future ahead of us. Both with good prospects and security for life but——' he shrugged again '—I respect your feelings and views. I just hope you don't live to regret what we had going for us.' His lips lightly brushed her forehead and he walked away.

Angel watched him and reflected that you couldn't regret what you'd never had. She might have had security with Patrick but that would have been all. With Hugo she'd tasted passion and an exhilaration she'd never tasted before, and if there were any regrets they were that she wouldn't taste them ever again.

Miles eyed her curiously as she entered their office suite on her first morning back after her spring break. Angel expected some sort of inquisition. She hadn't prepared an explanation for her behaviour in advance because she didn't know what Hugo had said to Miles when he had rung him that night.

'Good morning, Angel,' Miles said formally. 'Did you enjoy your break?'

'The weather was appalling,' was all she said as she sat at her desk and uncovered her computer. They were the first in, which was usual. For once Angel was glad of Miles's fairly strict office routine. If he said anything about Hugo she didn't want the rest of the penthouse staff to witness her misery.

'It often is at this time of the year.'

Angel gaped in surprise at his receding back as he walked into his office and closed the door behind him.

Was that it? With a small shiver she got up and went to the window. Yes, that was it, she thought mournfully as she stared out over the canal several floors beneath the penthouse suite of the Railton Group offices. Miles thought it was nothing. Hugo obviously did too, because although he had said he would call he had failed to ask her *where* he should call. He knew she worked here, but she held out no hope that he would contact her. Why should he?

She shrugged and went back to her desk. She was over two hurdles. Patrick had been dealt with and her boss was being discreet. One to go: Claudia. She had expected her to be at home when she'd got back from the Lake District but she hadn't been. She had phoned her aunt, Claudia's mother, who'd told her that Claudia was staying on in Corfu for a few more days, apparently having such a good time that she couldn't tear herself away.

So much for the broken-hearted syndrome that had been the basis of her depression. Claudia had made a remarkable recovery, but Angel knew that she herself would never get over what had happened on Summer Island. She had fallen in love with a callous villain; no money had changed hands but her heart had gone forever. She blamed herself entirely. She had known all about him and chosen to ignore it. She'd brought all this misery on her own head.

Her buzzer went and Angel went straight in to Miles. She was Miss Efficiency once more. They had a lot to get through with the opening of the new Riverside hotel so close. After that she would seriously consider London.

'So, I believe you've made the acquaintance of a friend of mine, Hugo Drake-Latimer,' Miles offered immediately. He was standing with his back to the window waiting for her.

Angel's heart fluttered desolately. So she hadn't got away with it as she had supposed. She'd always had a good working relationship with Miles. She knew little of his private life, apart from his wife who some-times dropped into the office when she was shopping in Manchester. They had two sons, both at university, and Miles played golf at the weekends. That was all she really knew about him. He was a good man to work for, kind and considerate, and they worked well together. She somehow felt that because of Hugo that relationship was tainted now, and her heart sank as she faced him.

Bravely she raised her chin. 'Yes, we met in the Lake District, in . . . in the hotel I was staying in,' she told him, thinking that if Miles knew where that phone call had come from he would challenge that. She had no idea what Hugo had said about her or how he had explained their meeting, but she couldn't deny that she had ever met him because Miles knew she had.

'You obviously made quite an impact on him,' Miles went on, his pale blue eyes holding hers across the office. 'Such an impact that he called me from the hotel for information about you.'

Angel's heart thudded with relief. So Hugo was discreet in some ways. That helped, but not very much. She was finding this all very embarrassing.

'Oh? What did you tell him?' she asked, as if she didn't know. A calm innocence was the best strategy, she decided.

'To be frank, I told him not to mess around with you.'

Angel's mouth dropped open. She hadn't expected that and Hugo had given her no idea. Was that why Miles had mentioned the message the trainee manager had left on everyone's computer? Angel pure, Angel bright. Implying that she was all virgin and unavailable.

'Th-thank you, but I...I can look after myself, Miles,' she told him, but from the way her voice faltered it didn't sound as if she could.

He smiled and came towards her. 'No woman can look after herself where Hugo is concerned,' he told her.

He sounded like a kindly father protecting an innocent daughter, and for a moment Angel rebelled at that. Did she come across as that vulnerable to everyone?

'I found him charming.'

'Oh, he is, Angel, I won't deny that, very charming, but...'

He paused, and in that short space of time Angel had time to think that he might have warned Hugo off her a few days ago, but now, at this precise moment, he was about to warn *her* off *him*.

'But he's a bit of a ladies' man and...'

And tell me something I don't know, Angel said to herself.

'...and I'm very fond of you and wouldn't like to see you hurt,' Miles finished.

I'm going to be an actress when I grow up, Angel thought childishly.

She smiled self-confidently, acting. 'Again, thank you for your concern, Miles, but it really wasn't that sort of meeting. We talked for a while, and he was charming. That was all.'

Miles nodded, looking relieved. 'I was worried about you, Angel. Hugo is a great friend but a bit eccentric and not really your sort and, well——' he shrugged slightly '—I was concerned for you, that's all.'

Angel acted out another smile of confidence though what was happening inside was the opposite. If she didn't know it already, Miles had confirmed it very nicely. Hugo wasn't her sort. Her sort was the good old dependable Patrick type. Damn Hugo Drake-Latimer, thief of hearts.

'Miles, can I ask you something?' Suddenly she wanted to salvage something out of this awful mess. Her self-confidence had taken a thrashing lately, and she really wanted to know if some of her judgement had been right and she wasn't a complete and utter fool where her instincts were concerned. 'Hugo has an investment company and he mentioned he had done business with you. I . . . I don't mean to pry but . . . but would you say he was trustworthy?'

Miles looked surprised. 'What an extraordinary question, Angel.'

'I know it must sound strange but . . .' Her mind raced feverishly. She hadn't thought beyond the initial question. 'Well, I . . . I have some savings and . . .' She took a deep breath. 'Well, actually my cousin, Claudia, has just lost a lot of money with . . . with an investment broker and——'

'And you're wary?' he finished for her. 'She should have invested it with Hugo,' he went on with a smile. 'He doesn't play Russian roulette with clients' money. He might be eccentric in many ways but not where money is concerned.' His grin widened, and Angel knew him well enough to know that he was confident that there was nothing between her and Hugo and it was spurring him to be more helpful. 'Where ladies' hearts are concerned he takes enormous risks, but never with money, Angel, never. If he's talked you into considering a small portfolio you can invest with confidence. Now, let's get on with the business of the day. We have a lot to get through before the opening of Riverside. Yes, a great deal.'

Later Angel considered what her boss had said about Hugo. A small weight had been lifted from her heart. Miles had confirmed what she had thought for herself: Hugo wasn't a villain. But the main weight from her heart hadn't shifted. He was a villain where hearts were concerned. There was no doubt of that.

CHAPTER SEVEN

MERCIFULLY the next week of Angel's life held only small pockets of time to think and regret and feel remorse for what she had done: allowed Hugo Drake-Latimer to change her life.

In fact he had changed very little of her working life. That trundled on as before, only slightly more hectic because of the imminent opening of the new hotel. The publicity people were working like slaves, getting the exposure the Riverside deserved, and arranging the enormous supper party that would launch it on its way.

Angel's home life wasn't so unaffected, though. There were times when she found her life so thoroughly miserable and desperate that even Outer Mongolia for a long holiday held appeal. Claudia wasn't back from Greece yet and Angel was feeling the loneliness of the town house they shared, but in one way she was glad of that loneliness because once her cousin was back Hugo would surely crop up in conversation at some time and she didn't want to hear about him or think about him.

He hadn't called the office, of course, but she hadn't really expected him to. Once she thought he might have called Miles, because when the call had come through on Miles's direct line her boss had dismissed her and carried on a conversation in very subdued tones. He didn't do that when his wife called! But maybe she had been clutching at straws, living in whimsy land again, thinking Hugo was checking to see if Miles knew anything about how she felt about him. Yes, whimsy land.

Angel flicked through a rail of extravagant cocktail dresses displayed in the most expensive frock shop this side of Paris. She chose a couple to try on and shivered slightly as she gazed at herself in the mirror wearing the first, a sleek sheath of black silk that was so superbly cut that it might have been custom-made for her.

'Fantastic,' the salesgirl breathed.

It was, fantastic. She felt so good in it... She bit her lip and stared at herself. She had changed, immeasurably so. Only weeks ago she wouldn't have considered this, buying such an extravagant dress that probably wouldn't ever get another airing after the opening of the new hotel. But she had changed, and whether for the long-term good she didn't know, but for the moment she didn't feel good at all. Her heart was breaking and in a way she had a conscience over Claudia. She hoped the feeling would pass, because outside she might look fantastic but inside she felt so bad.

'Angel.' Patrick called over the throng of people entering the foyer of the new Riverside hotel.

The place was festooned with silver and white bunting to match the interior furnishings. Local dignitaries had arrived, there were a few television celebrities floating about and the champagne was flowing.

Angel's heart sank as Patrick approached. Please don't let him want to patch things up, she silently prayed. He reached her side, pecked her cheek and gave her a light squeeze around the shoulders.

'I've been thinking, there's no need for us not to be friends just because we aren't an item any more. I must say this place has turned out to be superb.'

He gazed around the crowded foyer of the Riverside with admiration and Angel said a silent prayer of thanks. Just friends? It might work, but she suspected that Patrick had caught sight of her and had made a beeline for her as she was the first face he had recognised. She wondered if he would notice that she wore her hair down now. Her time with Hugo came flooding back to her, and all he had hinted about Patrick. Hugo knew how to make a woman feel like a woman, and though nothing had come of their relationship he had made her realise what she wanted from one.

'It is superb,' Angel agreed. 'Look, Patrick, I'll have to go. Miles needs me. There's a buffet in the conservatory overlooking the river and...' Her voice stilled and her heart turned to ice as she looked beyond Patrick to see...Hugo Drake-Latimer walking through the open doors of the foyer.

Patrick's arm was still around her shoulders, and as Hugo's eyes locked into hers across a sea of heads she felt an uncontrollable urge to flee from everyone and everything. And then her icy heart began to lurch dangerously. He wasn't alone; teetering after him came . . . Caroline.

Angel's colour drained with shock. Miles must have issued him with an invitation but her boss hadn't said, probably because he hadn't thought it necessary. As far as he knew they were nothing to each other, and Hugo was a friend and a bit of a celebrity, she supposed. But surely Hugo would have realised she would be here? All hope, if she had ever nurtured any, drained away with the colour in her face. If—just *if*— he had any feelings for her whatsoever he wouldn't have come with Caroline.

'I . . . I'll show you where the conservatory is,' she croaked to Patrick.

Patrick squeezed her shoulder lightly and then brushed a kiss across the side of her face which made her think the 'just friends' bit might be the prelude to starting over. Oh, God, she didn't need this.

'No need, you go ahead; I'll find it later and join you. I want to check that the computer system is working properly anyway. I really should have been here myself to supervise things but I can't be everywhere at once.' He chortled importantly, as if that might sway her back into their previous relationship.

Her heart hammering, Angel turned and streaked away herself. She headed for the conservatory, which ran the length of the hotel, overlooking the river. It was a stunning addition to the hotel, crammed with exotic foliage and white Victorian wrought iron. The terrace outside was lit with Victorian lamps casting pools of light over the gently flowing water of the river.

As yet there were only waiters and bar staff bustling around, giving the last finishing touches to the sumptuous buffet, and Angel caught her breath and desperately tried to still the thudding of her heartbeat. She needed recovery time to get over the horror of seeing Hugo, and the dreadful implication of that kiss Patrick had given her.

'Stunning.'

Angel whirled to face Hugo, shock-waves rushing the colour to her cheekbones. He looked superb in a white dinner-jacket and narrow black trousers. Her eyes fixed dazedly on the crimson Paisley silk bow-tie at his throat. It was so Hugo Drake-Latimer.

'Yes, it is,' she agreed in a small voice. 'The plants were imported from Venezuela and the Victoriana is genuine,' she rushed on.

'I was referring to you, not the surroundings.' His eyes grazed over her in a very intense perusal which thoroughly unnerved her.

It was a compliment, but the tone it was delivered in made it sound more like an insult. Angel wasn't sure how to take it. He must have dropped Caroline like a hot brick as soon as he had sighted her. But for the dark look in his eyes she might have experienced a small thrill at that. He looked angry, and because she had seen very little of his anger before she was very wary of it.

'Where's Caroline?' she asked, in control of her emotions once again. He had no right to feel any anger towards her.

'Where's Patrick?' he countered as if it was the last thing he wanted to know. 'I presume that was him draped around you in the foyer?'

If she hadn't known him and his reputation better she might have thought that that had been spoken with jealousy behind it. His attitude was certainly prickly.

'Networking,' she answered tightly, knowing that if she mentioned computers he would have something scathing to say about it. Computer buffs were probably crashing bores to a crime writer.

'If I were here with you I'd never leave your side.' His eyes penetrated hers so searchingly that she shivered inwardly.

'But you're not,' she said haughtily, and lifted her chin defiantly. 'You're here with Caroline.'

He raised a dark brow and his voice dripped pure cynicism. 'You noticed.'

Damn him! Why was he acting this way, almost spitefully?

'It's my place to notice the guests, being on the staff. So where is she? Don't tell me you've dumped her already?'

'I don't dump lady friends, Angel. But you certainly dropped Patrick very quickly on sight of me. What was it, guilty conscience?'

Angel couldn't believe the cruelty of him. How dared he make her feel so small when life was a game to him, and women mere playthings to be cast aside for a newer challenge?

She was so hurt that she went to brush past him, but he moved fractionally and it was enough to block her way. His hand grasped hers and his touch was electrifying. She snatched her hand back. 'I have to go.'

'You don't,' he challenged darkly.

Angel held her ground. 'What exactly do you want, Hugo?'

'I'd very much like a repeat of what happened on Summer Island,' he told her with candour.

The heat rose to her cheeks again. How easily he could embarrass her with his frankness, but once his forthrightness had excited her too; now it chilled her.

'No chance of that,' she uttered under her breath. A waiter was adjusting a table just beyond them and any minute now people would come flooding in for the buffet.

'Any reason?'

She shook her head in astonishment. 'Every reason, Hugo,' she said, keeping her voice low. 'What happened on your island was an aberration for me——'

'And me,' he interrupted abruptly, 'but all the same it was exquisite, sensuously, sexually erotic, and I enjoyed it so much I'd like to repeat it. Again and again.'

The coldness of the words shook her through and through. The content of what he said would once have filled her with desire and excitement but now...Miles's warning haunted her, the confirmation of what she had already known and ignored because she had let her heart fool her. Hugo was unscrupulous with women, a user of the worst sort—the sort that if ever you ran into him again you would be up against this sort of insult.

'I'm sure you say that to all your women!' It was the only weapon she had against him—a silly, churlish, not very original retort that only served to make her look a fool, not him.

His eyes flared and his hand snatched at hers again. The truth always hurt, she supposed, though he was hardly hurt, just angry that she hadn't fallen into his arms again like his other drippy women. She'd made one mistake—another definitely wasn't on the cards.

'Jealousy becomes you,' he grated as he urged her so close to him that she was maddeningly aware of his body heat. 'It gives a flash of colour to your cheeks that tempts me to prove I'm right.'

'And it doesn't take a master mind to work out what form that proof will take, does it?' she blurted rhetorically. 'My assessment of men crossing the threshold of hotels doesn't change, Hugo. You're all the same—sex-starved wildebeests——'

His mouth on hers shot the rest of her vitriol to the back of her throat. The pressure was intense, a punishment for getting her assessment right. Sex, that was all Hugo Drake-Latimer was interested in.

One arm was all that he needed to anchor her body hard against him. One kiss was enough to hurt so badly that she knew the pain would never go away. She couldn't even hate him because the positive side of her yearned for this to be the real thing, but the negative side overruled in the end as his mouth plundered hers so thoroughly that she could hardly breathe. He didn't care for her one bit, she reminded herself, because if he had he would have called, and he wouldn't have brought Caroline with him tonight, and he wouldn't have insulted her so deeply.

He drew back from her at last and she bit her lip in punishment for not having had the strength to do it herself. And as her senses regrouped she saw Patrick over Hugo's shoulder. He was among a crowd of other guests who had suddenly discovered the conservatory, and he had stopped at the sight of her in the arms of a man he didn't know, a man who had kissed her so thoroughly. He was watching them, his face drawn and hurt and obviously very shocked—and obviously thinking that Hugo was the reason she had ditched him so unexpectedly.

A desperate shame rushed through Angel then; it flooded her so completely that she felt a stirring of hate for Hugo and what he had done to her.

'I hope you're damned well satisfied now!' she blazed at Hugo, who looked at her as if she were demented. Then slowly he turned and saw Patrick across the conservatory. He showed no sign of remorse as he turned back to face her. 'You're not even sorry, are you?' she breathed passionately.

He gripped her wrists and stilled them, and because of Patrick's feelings Angel didn't move. Patrick probably couldn't see that he was gripping her and she didn't want to attract any more attention by struggling. The anger in her eyes did her battling for her.

'You're the one who should be sorry,' he told her with disdain. 'You're not so damned pure and bright, are you? That poor sap doesn't know what's coming to him.'

The tears stung the back of Angel's eyes. 'How dare you insult me?' she breathed quickly and hotly. 'How dare you speak to me like that?'

'I dare because it's all you deserve. I came here tonight because I knew you would be here, but what do I find? You in the arms of your lover, after what we were to each other——'

'Just a minute!' Angel blurted. Confusion ran riot inside her, banishing the protest that he was wrong and Patrick wasn't a part of her life any more. What on earth was he trying to say? And then suddenly she didn't want to know. He'd caused her enough trouble and pain.

'Go to hell, Hugo Drake-Latimer!' she breathed fiercely, and this time he could do nothing to restrain her. She pushed past him, nearly toppling a potted fern, and in her anger she swiped it with the back of her hand. It wasn't fair to take her wrath out on a harmless potted plant, but it was the plant or Hugo!

She flew out of the nearest door—there were several off the conservatory—and ran straight into Miles Wetherby, his wife Lorraine, and . . . and Caroline!

'Where's the fire?' Miles joked, the champagne and euphoria of the occasion obviously elevating his humour to a risky level.

'Miles, darling,' exploded Lorraine. 'That isn't funny. On the first night of the new hotel you could be tempting fate with jokes like that.'

They all laughed, but not Angel. She just burned as if *she* were on fire.

'Angel, meet Caroline, my wife's cousin. Caroline, this is my indispensable secretary, Angel Weston.

Behind every successful man is a woman—Angel is mine.'

Lorraine laughed and gave her husband a playful dig. 'I thought I was,' she protested with good humour.

They all laughed again and Angel felt her stomach tip dangerously. Caroline was laughing too and looking at her as if she had never seen her in her life before, which she hadn't, of course. She'd only had eyes for Hugo that night in the restaurant in the Lake District.

'Pleased to meet you, Angel,' Caroline enthused, quite genuinely to Angel's ears. 'What a sweet name. Are you one?'

Miles laughed, his pale eyes bright with mischief. 'Now there lies a story,' he said mysteriously. 'May I, Angel?'

Angel's heart bucketed but she gave a good show of indifference. What did anything in the world matter from now on?

'Be my guest. The rest of the world knows, why shouldn't you?' she directed wearily at Miles and Caroline, then, smiling at Miles's wife, she excused herself and left them.

She went straight to the manager's office to collect her wrap and her bag. She was going straight home. She wasn't wanted or needed here. She was nothing but the butt of Hugo's insults and the butt of people's jokes, and Patrick had looked at her as if she were Jezebel. She hoped they all had hangovers tomorrow morning. Hers had started already and not a drop had passed her lips!

* * *

Angel's heart sank when she heard the doorbell. She'd only just set foot inside the house. Surely not Patrick?

'Oh!' The exclamation came involuntarily as she opened the door. She'd braced herself to face Patrick but it was Hugo that faced her instead. The shock raced a thousand whys to her senses.

'Wh-what do you want?' she whispered hoarsely, clutching the side of the door fiercely. She could hardly think straight. Everything tumbled uselessly around her mind. He'd known where to find her. Had he always known she was his ex-lover's cousin? Was he expecting to find Claudia here, not her? What on earth did he want? To torment her more?

'I want to come in, for one thing,' he drawled, and boldly pushed open the door further and stepped into the hall. 'Nice place you have,' he commented drily, his eyes taking in the pale blue carpets and the rag-rolled walls. 'Is this going to be the happy marital home?' he added acidly.

Angel's heart raced as she closed the door after him. She had inquisitive neighbours across the courtyard, and if she hadn't she would have ordered him out.

'Well, is it?' he insisted, plunging his hands into his pockets and facing her.

She looked at him warily. He had never been here before; that was a certainty now. It seemed that his affair with Claudia had been conducted solely in hotel rooms. The thought of her cousin swamped her now and she felt a deep shame for what she had done. Why, oh, why hadn't she thought more of Claudia when she had been on Hugo's island? She had allowed herself to be bewitched by this man and all her moral upbringing and her good sense had gone to the wall. The power of the man . . . !

'I take your silence as confirmation that it will be,' he went on tightly.

Angel shook her head in dismay. 'N-no,' she breathed weakly. 'No, it isn't going to be the marital home. I...I'm not going to marry Patrick.' Once she'd said it she felt stronger, and angrier too. She didn't need this from him. She had enough emotion to cope with without him spiking at her so cruelly.

'How did you know where I live?' she asked.

'I didn't. I followed you here. It seems to be the trend these days.' His tone wasn't without sarcasm.

'So...so why?' she whispered. Indeed, why had he done that?

He took a deep breath and his eyes locked into hers. His expression was so strange that she felt her heart murmuring painfully.

'To apologise,' he said at last. 'I've behaved badly tonight——'

'It was no more than I expected from you,' she retaliated before he finished. She didn't believe for a minute that he had come to apologise. Her last words to him had been 'Go to hell', and that must have jolted his ego. He had probably expected her once more to fall into his arms as she had so stupidly done on his island. 'I don't want or need apologies from you, Hugo. I do want and need to forget your very existence.'

'Because everything is so good with you and Patrick now? They say a fling can strengthen a flagging relationship.'

What nerve. Bold as brass, he had marched into the Riverside with Caroline on his arm, and now he had the effrontery to goad her with Patrick. She was speechless. A great silence yawned till Hugo filled it.

'Is this the only room in the house?'

She said nothing but nodded towards the open door across the hall. He took his hands out of his pockets and went through. Angel followed, gathering strength from the release of pressure at facing him. He slumped down into one of the armchairs by the gas log fire which Angel had lit as soon as she had come in, needing warmth and a living flame to give her comfort. Now she wasn't feeling any form of comfort, though. Hugo looked too big for her little armchair. He didn't suit the confines of a terraced town house. He shouldn't be here.

'I'd like a drink,' he said.

Angel moved silently towards the sideboard. Claudia kept a few bottles here... Her hand seized the bottle of Scotch, the first bottle to hand, and guilt overwhelmed her. This was Claudia's home too. Poor Claudia, who had loved this man. It wasn't right! In anger she slammed shut the sideboard cupboard and straightened up.

'I don't want you to have a drink!' she blurted hotly. 'I don't want you here. I want you to go!'

With scarcely a movement he was on his feet and upon her and clutching at her shoulders as they shook with rage.

'I'm not going anywhere,' he told her firmly, his grip tightening. 'I want to be here because——'

'I know why you're here!' she scorned breathlessly. 'You told me back at the hotel. You . . . you think you can step back into my life and just . . . just bed me at will! How dare you say such things to me? How . . . how dare you take me for granted this way?'

'Listen to me,' he thundered. 'I said those things to you to jolt you into some sort of response. The first person I saw when I came through those doors was you in the arms of another man. The man you're planning on marrying——'

'I'm not going to marry him!' Angel blazed hotly. 'He hasn't asked me and he won't now anyway——'

He didn't let her finish. 'After he saw me kissing you? And you're sorry about that, aren't you?' he seethed angrily.

'No, no, I'm not sorry. I don't want to marry him. I don't want to see him again——'

'And you sure showed it, didn't you? This is what I can't understand about you. I thought you were different. I thought you were something so very special, but you're not. You've had long enough to sort out your affair with Patrick but you haven't, because you don't want to. Summer Island was nothing to you. You just drove out of my life and picked up with Patrick——'

'No! No, no, no!' Angel stormed fiercely. She could hardly register what he was saying but a small hope swelled—but she couldn't concentrate on that yet. He was thinking bad things of her that weren't true.

'Patrick and I are finished,' she went on heatedly.

'It sure as hell looked like it!'

Her shoulders tensed under his grasp. 'I'm not responsible for other people's actions,' she went on strongly. 'You saw what you wanted to see and you can believe what you want to believe. Anyway, it has nothing to do with you what I do with my life!'

His grip slackened slightly and the look in his eyes softened, confusing Angel.

'It is everything to do with me,' he said softly. 'I can't forget what happened between us.'

'Oh, no!' Angel exclaimed. 'Don't, just don't try and make out it was anything but what it was.'

'And what do you think it was? A brief encounter of the sexual sort, a last-minute fling for you before you settled down to wedded bliss?'

With all her strength she wrenched away from him. 'You creep!' she seethed. 'How dare you cheapen me this way when as soon as I left your damned island Caroline slotted herself back into your life? Don't deny it—I passed her in the car and then to-night...tonight you brought her to the reception, bold as you like——'

'Caroline is the cousin of your boss's wife. I've known her for years. She's a friend, that's all——'

'You call her darling,' Angel argued, wondering why she was putting all this before him. She didn't care any more; she just didn't.

'I call a lot of women darling. I call my mother, my sister, my sister's cat darling. It's a damned term of endearment that doesn't carry the weight and importance you seem to associate with it. I *accompanied* Caroline to the opening tonight because she didn't want to come alone. She's fresh out of a divorce and

I've been advising her what to do with her divorce settlement ...' He stopped suddenly and glared at her fiercely, and then his eyes went skyward. 'Why the hell,' he grated angrily, 'am I defending myself this way?'

Angel stared at him wide-eyed and suddenly very nervous. So why was he? Every pulse in her body jarred with a mixture of hope and fear. He must care, and that was why he was here. And she wanted him to care so very much, but ... but not this way, and not now, when her own life was in such a terrible mess.

'I want you to go,' she said huskily.

His eyes blazed one more time. 'No,' he said determinedly. 'I'm not going.'

Angel hugged her arms around her shoulders and stared at him, her eyes wide and tearless.

'I'm not going, not before I find out what makes you tick, Angel. I was furious with you tonight, furious because you were with Patrick and I didn't expect you to be.'

Angel's brow rose in mock-surprise. 'And you have expected too much, Hugo,' she said quietly.

She wanted to hurt him for this because if he had called, if he hadn't let her out of his life so easily, it would all have been all right. But no, how could it ever be right? Miles had warned her about him, and she knew first-hand from Claudia how he treated women. She didn't want to be treated like all the others.

Still hugging herself for comfort, still suffering because of him, she went on, 'I acted out of character with you. I allowed the excitement of the situation

and your charm to ruin everything I cherished and
held dear to my heart. You bewitched me into your
bed and I feel a deep shame for that. I couldn't have
continued with Patrick after what I did. I couldn't
have continued with any man after that. I thought I
loved Patrick till I met you and went crazy. You ruined
all that for me——'

'He wasn't right for you.'

'He would have been,' Angel argued.

It wasn't the truth. Now she knew that it would
never have worked. She hadn't loved him enough, because if she had she wouldn't have fallen for Hugo
so easily. But she couldn't tell him that.

'We would have been all right,' she went on. 'But
I don't blame you. I blame myself, and at this moment
I'm not very proud of myself. I have a conscience for
what I've done. You seem to think I'm some sort of
Jezebel, doing what I did with you and then coming
back to Patrick. Well, it's not true. I'm not like that.'

Her eyes were wide and appealing but the tears were
dangerously close.

'So you had every intention of finishing with him
for me?' he questioned softly.

Did she detect hope in his voice?

Not now, she thought desperately. I can't cope with
you caring now. I'm suffering too much.

'Because of you,' she corrected him quietly. She felt
no anger or rage now, just the sorrow that was inevitable with a man like him. 'Because of what we
did together. Although Patrick and I didn't have a
firm commitment we were an item. We had a mutual

respect for each other and what I did was as good as being unfaithful.'

'Rubbish,' he grated. He stepped towards her and Angel visibly flinched. He stopped. 'There's something else, more to this than meets the eye, and I want to get to the root of it. We made love on my island, not sex, love——'

'Stop it!' Angel cried, backing away from him. She didn't want him to touch her because she would be lost if he did. 'We didn't make love, we did what animals——'

He caught her wrist and wrenched her into his arms. 'Don't ever say such things again; don't ever think them!'

She struggled but it was hopeless. 'You didn't even call me,' she blurted tearfully. 'Not one word, not one!'

He held her then, tightly and passionately against him, grazing kisses across her hair. 'Is this what it's all about? Dear God, Angel, I gave you breathing-space to get your life with Patrick in order. I needed space myself to get my own life in order. Life doesn't just stop after what happened to us. I'm crazy about you.'

His mouth found hers and her world skidded again, perilously. Desire flooded her before anything else and she knew how dangerous that was. The temptation was there again and she so badly wanted to rebel against it because the doubts and fears were crashing all around her again. But his magic was too much for her, dashing all reasoning, bringing her down to that unacceptable level of need which was destroying her.

But in spite of everything she let herself go and wound her arms around him, trembling now as his kisses deepened, and his desire was all that was needed to dash all and everyone else in the world from her mind.

CHAPTER EIGHT

HUGO drew her on to the rug in front of the fire, pressing her down with kisses of fire, caresses of desire.

She moaned in his arms and he comforted her as if she were suffering a fever.

'I don't want to hurt you, Angel,' he breathed softly.

'But you are,' she insisted.

'In what way?'

She tried to struggle up but he wouldn't allow it.

'I don't know,' she murmured miserably, but she did. His timing was all wrong. How could she believe anything he said when Miles's warning still echoed in the chambers of her heart? Now she could see why that warning had been issued. Caroline was his wife's cousin, fresh out of a divorce, looking for an eligible bachelor, and she'd found one, and no two-bit secretary of his was going to interfere. And Claudia, also a wealthy divorcee, had been cheated out of her heart and her fortune by him. Angel had allowed this man to plough through her emotions and sensibilities where her cousin was concerned. She shouldn't have allowed that to happen. What sort of a person was she?

'Let me go,' she pleaded, looking up at him sprawled over her.

He gripped her wrists and held her arms above her head on the rug. His eyes were dark and determined.

'I can't let you go,' he murmured. 'I don't want to let you go. I want to understand you but I don't. We have something and you're fighting it and I want to know what it is. If it's Patrick, tell me one time that it's him you want and——'

'And you'll let me go?' She was tempted to lie to him, to tell him that Patrick was her life, not him, but she couldn't.

'No, I'll fight for you, the only way I think I can.' He lowered his mouth to hers and the kiss was so wretchedly, damnably persuasive that her insides somersaulted dizzily. She didn't want this sort of pressure. It was wrong and so unfair. She wanted time to analyse what he was trying to say but he wasn't giving her that space.

He slid the fine straps of her dress down, and his mouth on the naked flesh of her shoulder was as hot as a branding-iron. She could hardly breathe with the delicious agony of it.

'Oh, no,' she uttered weakly. 'I don't want you to do this.'

'You do,' he murmured silkily as he grazed kisses across her throat. 'You want me as badly as I want you. We matter, not anyone else, just us and how we feel. I love you, Angel.'

Her heart sprang within her fragile ribcage. He loved her? Had she heard right? Was this another of her fantasies?

His kisses were fire on her throat, then fire on her own burning lips. He was crushing her with his power,

breaking her down till she was weak with the onslaught on her emotions. She knew in her heart that
this was how love should be, wanting so badly that
it cancelled out all sensible reasoning. Her careering
mind with its tousled thoughts of wrongs was spinning
so dizzily that it was like a drug. Love was a drug,
and Hugo's love an overdose of the most delicious
sort. She succumbed completely, lost in wave after
wave of need and hope.

She clung to him and thought he sighed a sigh of
relief, but how could she trust her judgement any
more? Her lips parted for him, her heart flowered for
him. They wanted and needed each other and that
was all that mattered.

Her dress, his evening suit, her conscience were no
barriers now. She felt the heat of his hands on the
smooth flesh of her thighs above her silk stockings,
and her pulses throbbed at the low groan of submission that came from his lips.

'Dear God, but you are a mystery, Angel pure,' he
breathed heavily. 'You dress like an avenging angel,
pure sensuality. You drive me crazy.'

And he was driving her crazy with his caresses that
blazed trails of molten fire wherever he touched. Their
mouths were a frenzy of love and desire, searching
and finding and devastating in the power they wielded.
His arousal was hard against her groin, and then he
moved into her and the skill with which he accomplished it had her gasping with surprise. And then
there were no more shocks as he moved inside her.
Just sweet, sensational feelings as he moved and
crushed her lips with the power of his love. She felt

it, his love, for the way he moved so divinely could only be love, nothing else. She encompassed him, drew him deeper and deeper into her secret self, drawing moans of pleasure from his lips and pressing small gasps of joy to her own.

Their climax when it came was hot and fiery, rushing at them from a flurry of short, sharp thrusts, devastating in the uncontrolled way it exploded like thunder on a hot summer's day, unexpected, unruly, pounding with the pent-up thrust of needed relief.

And the rush of Angel's tears as they lay exhausted in each other's arms came with the calm after the storm of raging emotions.

'I hate you for that,' she moaned helplessly, clinging to him none the less.

'I hate myself for it,' he moaned sympathetically, and twisted her in his arms so that he could look down into her flushed face.

She squeezed shut her eyes so that he wouldn't see her despair, but the tears smearing down her cheeks were obvious enough.

'It's how it is sometimes,' he said tenderly. 'Urgent and passionate——'

'We . . . we still have our clothes on,' Angel sobbed with shame.

He held her close and smoothed her hair and she thought he must be laughing at her for her naïveté. 'It doesn't matter,' he soothed. 'It really doesn't.'

'It matters to me,' she blurted, stronger now, more deeply ashamed than ever, and it was all his fault. She struggled out of his arms and pushed down her dress, but his hands stilled her. He pressed her gently down again and propped himself up on one elbow to look down into her tear-stained face.

'It was the stockings that did it, Angel. They arouse me enormously.'

There was humour in his tone and she didn't think it funny. She looked up at him with dismay clouding her eyes. 'Sex,' she breathed raggedly. 'It's just sex to you.'

His eyes darkened momentarily and then he smiled as if he understood. 'Yes, sweet one, sex . . .' She struggled again, her heart hammering, feeling so terribly cheated and hating him for that. He held her tightly, so determinedly that her strength ebbed alarmingly quickly. 'Sex and love and desire,' he went on. 'And there's nothing wrong with it, nothing at all.'

'Life's rich pattern, I suppose,' she spat contemptuously.

'Yes, life's rich pattern,' he agreed solemnly. 'You really are Angel pure, Angel bright, aren't you? I can see I'm going to have to teach you the ways of the world.'

'I don't want to know them,' she fought back.

'You loved it, Angel——'

'You wretched cavalier!'

He laughed and bent to kiss her lips and she wanted to bite him or something but the sweet pressure was too much for her.

'You see,' he said tenderly after he had drawn back from her. 'You haven't been cheated; you just think you have because you don't understand.'

'I understand that what we just did——'

'Was beautiful and compulsive and erotic and it's how it is between two people who love each other.'

'You take a lot for granted!'

She couldn't even annoy him. He was still gazing down at her, sublimely confident that she did love him though she hadn't said it. Perhaps spoken words didn't matter to him—perhaps her body had said all he needed to know. Damn her wretched body. Damn him.

She struggled up from the floor and he did nothing to stop her this time. With trembling hands she smoothed down her dress and glared down at him. His bow-tie lay beside him on the floor and his shirt was half undone but everything else was intact, and she thought how suave of him it was not to be suffering any indignity when she blazed with embarrassment at the sight of her lacy briefs peeking out from under the sofa.

He got to his feet and stood before her, his eyes darkly serious. 'Will you talk to me now, Angel?' He rested his hands on her bare shoulders and even after all that had happened she was aware of the fiery contact of their flesh.

She loved him so very much. It squeezed at her heart and made her feel breathless. She was mad with him and ashamed of her wanton behaviour and yet she knew it was still her conscience stabbing at her relentlessly. She loved a con man, the man who had cheated her cousin in the name of research and even for some sort of twisted thrill, and yet Miles had told her he was trustworthy. Oh, she didn't understand him or herself, and how could she trust him? He said he loved her but did she believe it? She wanted to, but there were too many other nasty issues battling for her reasoning. She should be feeling ecstatic but she didn't. A huge black cloud of doubts and unanswered questions hung over her, dulling all euphoria from her mind.

She rubbed her forehead and then let her hand drop to her side. 'I . . . I can't think of a relationship with you at the moment,' she went on. She needed time to clear this mental debris from her mind.

She lifted her chin and gazed straight into the eyes of the man she loved. He wouldn't know it—she couldn't tell him that she had probably fallen in love with him on sight. She had to let him go. This decision, unbidden and shot out from her conscience, was the only way. She couldn't live like this. She had to let him go.

'Patrick is still in your heart,' he grated quietly.

His eyes had taken on a lacklustre blankness and it stabbed cruelly at Angel's heart. He did care, but maybe not as much as he thought he did. Men like him didn't hurt easily. She reminded herself of Claudia and how he had treated her, and she suffered more pangs of remorse for not considering her cousin more deeply before.

'You don't realise what you've done to me, Hugo. You fill me with shame, my shame for what I've done with you——'

'I don't want to hear this——'

'Well, you're going to,' she insisted, but of course she couldn't tell all. Perhaps if she tried to explain about Patrick it would be enough. 'I've still got a conscience over Patrick but I wouldn't have if you hadn't come into my life... OK, OK, I know it was I that came into your life but I didn't know what was going to happen. You made me realise that marriage to Patrick would be an empty shell and I'm grateful for that, but I hurt him because of you...' Her shoulders sagged beneath his hands and he let her go. 'We had an understanding and, though he hadn't said, he expected to marry me.'

'He's that predictable,' Hugo grazed scathingly.

Angel nodded. 'Yes, he's that predictable and...and you're not and you worry me and——'

'You want me out of your life,' he finished for her.

Her eyes widened painfully but she couldn't deny it. She thought she saw anger then, in the darkness of his eyes and the tensing of his jawline.

'Very dangerous, Angel,' he stated threateningly. 'You can play around with anyone else's emotions but mine. I won't stand for it. What you did with me on the island and now, tonight, doesn't come across as the actions of a person who has any thought for anyone but herself——'

'Don't, Hugo,' she pleaded. 'It isn't like that.'

'Isn't it? I'm beginning to get the message but it isn't a very pleasant one. I think there's a name for your sort and it's a far cry from the "Angel pure" label I've been hearing so much about...'

Oh, God, it was getting worse, this terrible condemnation of her actions from him when she was already punishing herself for them. Now Hugo thought all evil of her, and Patrick did too, and Claudia would if she ever found out.

He bent and snatched his tie up from the rug and thrust it around his neck. His eyes were black as they settled on hers.

'I'm not waiting around for you to clear your false conscience,' he went on gravely. 'Go back to Patrick and your safe, predictable life with him and forget you're a whore at heart. I won't!'

The insult slammed into her so painfully, it was like a bullet wound to her heart. She stepped back in shock, her face white, her eyes burning. Hugo swept past her.

The door slammed behind him and the walls seemed to close in on her. The silence that followed his furious exit was so crippling that she sank to her knees and covered her face in despair.

'Fantastic tan,' Angel complimented brightly the following day when Claudia returned from her holiday.

'To hell with the tan,' Claudia grumbled as she shut the front door with a resounding wallop.

Angel's much laboured heart plummeted like a block of concrete in a still pool. The holiday had given Claudia's skin a healthy glow but not penetrated very deeply into her depression. She followed her into the kitchen where Claudia set about pouring the coffee that Angel had just made for herself.

'How was it?' Angel asked tentatively, taking the cup of coffee that Claudia slid across the work surface to her.

'Greece? Greece is Greece and the sun is the sun——'

'You still feel bad,' Angel uttered, wondering what she could offer her cousin for comfort. It was obvious that the holiday had been a waste of time. Angel felt for her—now she knew first-hand what it was like to have loved and lost.

'I feel like hell,' Claudia retorted sharply as she slumped down on to a kitchen chair. 'The flight was delayed for four hours and then my bags went astray at Manchester airport. Story of my life at the present— mind-bending chaos!'

'I'm sorry,' Angel offered, totally inadequately. Life was a bitch one way and another.

'Do you feel like getting drunk?' Claudia suggested, and then looked away from Angel. 'No, you don't get drunk, do you? I'll have to do it solo.' She got up, went into the sitting-room and came back with the bottle of Scotch, the one Angel had slammed back into the sideboard the night before.

It hit Angel then. If only Claudia hadn't gone away, if only she had been here during Angel's spring break, she wouldn't have taken off for the Lakes, she would never have met Hugo and...

She shivered as if someone were walking over her grave as Claudia poured herself a Scotch.

'You...you still love him, don't you?' Angel said as Claudia took a gulp. She didn't really want to hear it all again, the pain and suffering of losing a lover, but perhaps now that she had more insight into the vagaries of love she could offer some sort of comfort. It would be excruciatingly painful for her, but it was the least she could do for her cousin to listen again till Claudia exorcised him from her mind.

'Huh! Love. What's love? You know, I did a lot of thinking while I was away,' Claudia went on. 'There must be something sadly lacking in my life for me to have fallen for that creep.'

Angel understood that. There obviously had been something lacking in her life for her to have fallen for him as well.

'I mean, I allowed him to sweep me off my feet as if I were some giddy teenager.'

'Yes, I know,' murmured Angel in agreement, truly knowing.

'I can't believe I actually fell for that investment scam as well. He must have thought I was some dumb bimbo. That's what really gets to me, you know, the real pain, being taken for a ride like that.'

'He...he could have lost your money legitimately,' Angel volunteered. 'The money market is a funny business, Claudia. He...might have just been unlucky and because he failed you he was too embarrassed to...to carry on the affair.'

Claudia shook her head. 'No, no way. I had time to think while I was away, really think. He swept me off my feet that night we met in a bar, and then the wining and dining and that weekend in Paris. He'd set it all up from the start and I fell for it.' She took another drink and then smiled. 'He thinks he's going to get away with it but he isn't—oh, no. I'm back now, fully recovered and in control and out for vengeance.'

Angel stared at her in dismay. Claudia had a new determination about her, a new dangerous determination, as if she had some horrible plan for Hugo's future.

'V-vengeance?' she breathed nervously.

'Yes, Angel, vengeance. Sweet revenge.' She took another mouthful of Scotch, placed the empty tumbler down on the table in front of her and squeezed it tightly as if it might be Hugo Drake-Latimer's throat.

Angel felt prickles of fear running down her spine.

'I hate him, Angel. I hate him for making a fool out of me. I hate him for stealing my money. He's probably doing the very same thing to some other poor, hapless female at this very moment. Wining and dining her, declaring his undying love for her. Well, not for much longer.' She smiled wickedly, her eyes slightly glazed.

'Claudia, what...what are you going to do?' Angel whispered fearfully.

Claudia looked at her, still smiling. 'I'm going to bed actually. That flight home was a nightmare.' She hauled herself to her feet and Angel stared at her helplessly.

'Claudia, what are you going to do?' Angel repeated, her voice rising in anguish.

Claudia frowned. 'What do you think I'm going to do?'

'I don't know,' Angel bleated impatiently. 'You're tipsy; you're not thinking rationally——'

'I'm not tipsy, just thoroughly exhausted, and I'll tell you what I'm going to do. I'm going to do what I should have done when I first found out I'd been cheated. I'm going to the police——'

'You can't!' Angel wailed. Her pulses raced so hard she felt faint. Oh, God, she couldn't go the police. It would ruin Hugo.

'I can and I will,' Claudia stated firmly as she turned from the door to look at Angel. 'He cheated me and he's got to be stopped.'

Angel went to her and placed her hand on her arm. Her eyes were wide and pleading. She had to try and stop her somehow.

'Why now, Claudia? Before, you said that you'd have no chance of getting him back if you went to the police.'

A rueful smile turned the corners of Claudia's mouth. 'That was when I thought I was in love with him, Angel.' She sighed. 'Love never works out when it erupts so swiftly. It was infatuation, that's all.' She placed her hand warmly over Angel's. 'What you and Patrick have is the real thing. A love born of friendship and trust, uncomplicated and easy. You're a lucky girl, Angel.'

Lucky girl! She couldn't be more unlucky if she tried, Angel thought. Claudia was wrong about love never being the real thing when it erupted so swiftly. What Angel's heart was going through now was far from ephemeral. It was a love that would live through whatever life threw up at her in the future. Unfulfilled love, though.

A deep sigh shuddered through Angel as she cleared the coffee-cups. There was no hope for a future with Hugo but she loved him enough to want to try and do something for him. But what? Warn him that Claudia was out for revenge? She didn't even know where to contact him—only the cottage on the lake, and she didn't know the phone number.

Maybe when Claudia had slept off her exhaustion she could persuade her to reconsider ... or maybe persuade Hugo to return her money. He didn't need it. He wasn't a crook, not a real one. He just couldn't be.

CHAPTER NINE

THE following week exploded around Angel in a fury. It had started uncertainly with Claudia going down with a bug she had picked up on her holiday, which confined her to bed and bathroom in rapid succession. In a way Angel blessed the bug. Claudia was so weak and wan that it drove revenge out of the window for the time being.

The Riverside hotel was suffering teething problems and Miles had been over there all week trying to bring calm to chaos, and Angel was left in the penthouse office trying to carry on as if all were well with the world.

Her formal resignation still lay on Miles's desk, as yet unopened because Miles wasn't here. And the anticipation of his reaction when he eventually came back and opened it had given her a permanent, thudding headache all week.

And a snarl-up in the computer system was probably on the cards, Angel thought negatively as the weekend approached, and Patrick would need to be called out, and facing him again was something she didn't want.

There you go, Angel breathed to herself, acting out of character again. Where was her cool, calm efficiency now? Panicking over something that wasn't going to happen. There was absolutely nothing wrong with the computers.

She poured herself a cup of coffee in her outer office when everyone had disappeared to lunch, and her hands shook fearfully as she did it. It just needed Hugo to walk in now and she would go to jelly.

'Make that two,' a voice thundered from behind her.

The coffee-cup slid from her fingers and bounced on the thick-pile carpet at her feet. She swung round, her heart hammering viciously inside her breast.

'Hugo!' Her eyes widened in dazed shock. He had no reason to be here, none at all.

He bent down and picked up the cup from her feet and handed it to her. He wore a formal suit but he looked drained in it. He looked as if he had all the troubles of the world on his Savile Row shoulders. He looked angry, too.

Angel acted on her emotions swiftly and surely. She controlled them with a great resurgence of sense. It was finished, her brief affair with this man. She didn't love him; it was infatuation and she would get over it—eventually.

'Wh-what do you want?' she uttered. Surely he hadn't sought her out, unable to live his life without her?

'Information, actually. But before you get it for me, don't you think you ought to mop up that coffee before it spoils the carpet?'

For a second she stared at him and then, tightening her lips into a narrow line of annoyance, she tore off a handful of kitchen roll and scrubbed at the carpet.

'Satisfied?' she blurted as she tossed the stained, crumpled paper into the nearest bin.

'I was once—or was it twice?' He shrugged. 'How could I forget? It was three times to be precise, three times we've made love.'

'Three times too many,' Angel retorted, and poured more coffee, her fingers tense at the blunt reminder of what to her had been a three-times voyage of hedonistic pleasure and discovery. 'Do you still want coffee?'

'Of course.'

She poured him one. 'Why are you so scathing with me, Hugo?' she asked quietly as she handed it to him. 'It's not very macho, you know.'

He smiled cruelly. 'I can't help it. The man scorned and all that. I don't take too kindly to being thrown over for a lesser man than myself.'

'So you did come here to torment me?' she accused mildly. She wasn't going to lose her temper with him; that would show that she cared.

'No, I came for information from Miles—and why not a bit of Angel-baiting while you get me that information?'

'Angel-baiting, eh? I would have thought you above that sort of thing.'

'I'm not above anything if I get what I want in the end.' His eyes bored into hers, heavy with meaning, heavy with an anger that worried her.

Choosing to ignore what he really meant, she turned the meaning of his words in another direction. What information was he talking about?

'Miles hasn't been here all week and I'm not expecting him today. He's dealing with some problems at the Riverside hotel. Is there anything I can do for you?'

He smiled cynically, that was all, but it was enough to send the colour rushing to her throat. She left herself wide open at times. Unpredictably he made no sarcastic reference to her query.

'Does the name Ralph Arnott mean anything to you?'

Angel finished her coffee and placed the cup on the table behind her. She concentrated on the name, only vaguely wondering why he should ask. The trouble was that when he was standing so close to her nothing but his sensuality was alive to her. Would she ever get over him? He was never out of her thoughts.

'No, I don't think so. Should it?'

'Possibly not. He's an ex-employee of this company, according to my head of personnel. Up until a couple of weeks ago he worked for my company but unfortunately he's disappeared. To say that I'm keen to trace him would be a mild understatement,' he added contemptuously.

He placed his empty coffee-cup next to Angel's, and she watched as his hand went up to knead his brow impatiently. It was a gesture she hadn't seen before. On his island he had been so laid-back, untroubled, unconcerned. He looked fraught and angry now, and it was highly gratifying to think it might be because of her. Her heart softened at the delicious thought. He'd admitted his love and she had thrown it back at him but, though it had crucified her to do it, it had been the only way. But no, he was worried about one of his employees, not her. It showed he had a certain caring for someone else, though.

On this new wave of sympathy and remorse for the hurt she *might* have caused him, she made a suggestion that would have horrified Miles if he'd been there.

'P-perhaps I can help. We keep files on ex-employees. Jeanette, our personnel officer, is away at the moment but I'm sure I can——'

'I'm sure you can. I want that classified information and now. I've a busy schedule,' Hugo said tightly.

Angel felt stung by his abruptness. Her helpful suggestion had been spurred by an absurd need to keep him here, but it was obvious he didn't want to be. What a fool she was over this man. She steeled her heart and strengthened her position of trust with Miles. No one was allowed access to those files without permission.

'Miles wouldn't——'

'Miles would. Now, will you get me what I want or do I have to waste time finding them for myself?'

It wasn't really a suggestion, just determination to get what he wanted regardless. Angel wavered. He and Miles were friends and maybe Miles had given his permission. She didn't know but she wasn't going to battle with him over something so trivial. Reluctantly she headed for Jeanette's office, throwing over her shoulder as she went, 'I suppose it's all right, seeing as you're practically family now.' She didn't attempt to hide the sarcasm in her tone.

'And what do you mean by that?' he barked as he followed her out of the office and into the adjoining one.

'I don't need to elaborate, Hugo,' she said as she seated herself at Jeanette's console and proceeded to operate her computer.

'Caroline?'

Angel shrugged dismissively and immediately felt a strong hand on the back of her neck.

'Caroline is a friend, not a lover. I thought I made that clear.' His voice was deep and thick.

His touch turned to a caress and heat careered down Angel's spine. One touch and she was molten fire, wanting him and wishing that life weren't so muddled and complicated. The screen in front of her blurred.

'Don't do that, Hugo,' she pleaded.

'I like it and you do too,' he said, but his voice was bitingly cruel. She felt him release the clip that was holding up her hair. 'And I prefer your hair down, not up; it's far sexier.'

'And this isn't the movies,' she retorted grimly, trying to swing her head out of his reach.

His hand was firmly entwined in her hair and she was trapped. He held her still and moved slightly round her chair, and before she knew it his mouth was on hers. She suffered his lips on hers, tried in vain to despise him because the kiss was a punishment, not a sign of caring. But the pressure was too much for her, gripping her heart with love and squeezing it till it was dry.

He drew back at last. His eyes were dark. 'So you still care,' he murmured sarcastically. 'That's a surprise—but then again maybe not. Angel pure is quite accomplished at running two affairs simultaneously, isn't she?'

The insult jarred but she was getting used to it. She glared up at him. 'I'm sure if Angel pure were here herself she could think of a cryptic retort to that,' she countered stiffly.

Hugo smiled wryly. 'You talk of her as if she weren't you.'

'No, Hugo, you do. I never made that claim; someone else did. Someone as resentful and cruel as you.'

She glared back at the computer screen, determined to ignore his insults and that kiss he had inflicted so punishingly on her lips.

As she scrolled employees' details across the screen, something in the back of her mind responded, jangling at her memory bank. Angel pure, Angel bright. Hugo's reference to Angel pure was niggling at her, but not for the reason of his insult, something else.

'This is probably a waste of time,' Hugo said impatiently behind her. He had been watching the screen over her shoulder, leaning one hand on the back of the chair, so close to her that she could feel the whisper of his breath on the top of her head. 'My head of personnel will have the same information as your files.'

'So why bother Miles with this?' Angel asked vaguely, concentrating on what she was doing because if she didn't his breath on the top of her head would cause her to hyperventilate again.

'Because I've never met the guy and I hoped your files would give more information than my own.'

'How can you employ the man and not know him?'

'Easily, when you're torn between two professions.'

She remembered that he'd said he delegated a lot now and his writing was taking over his life.

'What's he done, run off with the petty cash?' Angel snapped back.

There was a silence and then a bitter laugh from Hugo. 'I wish.'

'Aha!' Angel exclaimed, and it all came back to her. 'Ralph Arnott!' She couldn't believe the coincidence. It was astonishing.

'So you do know him.'

Angel studied the details she'd brought up, still not quite believing that the man Hugo was seeking was this one. 'He insisted on being called Ross; that's why the name didn't ring a bell before,' she gabbled on. 'I suppose he thought Ross was more appealing to women than Ralph.'

Angel swivelled round to face Hugo who was gazing past her at the details on the screen.

'Angel pure, Angel bright,' she murmured. 'He's the trainee manager Miles sacked some while back.'

Hugo said nothing, but his eyes blazed angrily. He straightened up.

'How well did you know him?' he asked.

'Not very well. He was only here a short time and I didn't have much cause to associate with him, and when I did he was always making suggestive remarks and trying to... Well, you know.'

'A womaniser?'

'Yes,' Angel admitted. It was probably why she hadn't remembered his surname. Men like Ross were instantly forgettable.

'Give me that file,' he ordered darkly.

His seriousness frightened her. She stalled for time, time she needed to consider whether she ought to let him have it or not. She'd be in trouble if Miles hadn't given his permission.

'Wh-why do you need to trace him?' she asked. She was curious now that she knew who he was, curious to know why Hugo was so angry.

'Never you mind,' he grated. 'It's taught me a salutary lesson, though. Never turn your back for fear of silver blades in the night.'

Angel's mouth went dry. Was that a cryptic dig at her for what he thought she had done to him?

She didn't know and she wasn't about to find out. He leaned forward, took the file and without another word stormed from the office.

And that was it.

Angel heard the outer door close after him, very finally. He hadn't even looked back. Her fingers went to her lips; she could still feel the pressure of his mouth on hers and she supposed she always would. She'd never see him again and the loss squeezed her heart.

'Come on, Angel. It will do us both good. You've been so sweet to me all week, looking after me and listening to all my miseries. I've been so selfish when you've had your own miseries to contend with. You should have told me about your split with Patrick before instead of bottling it up,' Claudia remonstrated as she sat in front of the dressing-table mirror putting the last touches to her make-up.

Angel was sitting on her hands on the edge of Claudia's bed, watching her. Claudia's suggestion that they go out for a meal had been instigated by Angel's confession that she and Patrick had parted. The confession had come because Claudia had pushed for some sort of explanation for Angel's paleness and lethargy. Angel had tried to pass it off as pressure of work and worry over Claudia's bug, but her cousin hadn't been satisfied.

'It's man trouble, isn't it?' she'd insisted knowingly, and Angel had known she could never confess to the *real* man trouble, never in a million years. So she'd told her about Patrick and Claudia had nodded sagely as if she were the expert on torn hearts, and now she had come up with her remedy for the blues— a girls' night out. Angel balked at the thought, let alone the actuality of it.

'I don't feel like going out,' Angel told her morosely, and was about to plead exhaustion but Claudia didn't give her the chance.

'Look, Angel, sitting in fretting does no good——'

'Huh, great advice coming from one who knows, I suppose.'

Claudia turned round to her and smiled. 'OK, I've been an absolute idiot over that creep, but you made me see that I must put it all behind me. You've persuaded me not to go to the police but to put the affair down to experience and forget it. Well, the same applies to yourself, Angel. Forget Patrick and let me treat you to a meal at the Riverside. I'm aching to see the place after all you've told me.' She swung back to the mirror. 'Come on now, get your glad rags on and let's go out for a bit of rehabilitation. God knows, we both need it.'

Reluctantly Angel shifted herself off the bed and into her own bedroom. Yes, she needed some rehabilitation but in an isolation hospital for broken hearts, not the wretched Riverside hotel where memories were lurking ready to strike.

She raked her hands through her unruly hair, wondering if she had the strength actually to get ready and go out. Yes, she had talked Claudia into not going to the police over Hugo's scam. It had been no mean feat. In her heart she knew the man should be exposed if he was a crook, but Hugo wasn't, surely? It wasn't in his nature. Womanising was but not the fraud. So all was right in Claudia's world at last, but Angel wondered about herself. Would she ever get over Hugo Drake-Latimer?

'Oh, it's wonderful,' Claudia enthused as they sat in the bar of the Riverside later, sipping Martinis and waiting to order. 'Fantastic menu, too.'

'We're lucky to get a table,' Angel commented absently, glancing across the bar to the long conservatory that was already crowded with diners. The memory was already niggling at her nerves. She hoped they wouldn't be ushered to that table by the potted ferns where Hugo had . . .

Angel's face blanched and her stomach rolled sickeningly. The table was already occupied. A lone diner, though the table was set for two. Hugo Drake-Latimer sat gazing out over the floodlit terrace and the river beyond. He looked a thousand miles away and Angel wished she really were—far from here, on another planet, would do just fine!

Dear God, if Claudia saw him! Her whole life, past and present, rolled before her eyes. This was her punishment, God's own punishment for her sins. She should have told Claudia the truth—that she wasn't pale and distraught over Patrick but suffering acutely for falling in love with the man Claudia herself had fallen so painfully for.

Panic surged the next words to her lips. 'This is ridiculous, Claudia,' she blurted, snatching the menu that her cousin was drooling over. 'You can't possibly eat anything on that menu. You've been in bed all week with a bug. A prawn cocktail will play havoc with your digestive system.'

With a giggle Claudia snatched it back. 'Let me be the judge of that, sweetie. I'm so hungry I could eat my way through the——'

'Why, hello! It's Angel, isn't it?'

Angel turned, her blood already running cold on recognition of the voice. She gazed up into the radiant face of Caroline. Angel's mind went into a spin and the room swam all around her. A table for two, Hugo waiting expectantly... She'd thought things couldn't be worse and now they were, so painfully worse that she wanted to die.

'You do remember me, don't you? We met very briefly at the opening. You work for Miles——'

'Y-yes, of course, C-Caroline,' Angel stuttered, and leapt to her feet, wanting to run but knowing her legs wouldn't carry her very far. They were like jelly sticks. Her mouth worked automatically, though, primed by a lifetime of doing the right thing—although that had hardly helped her where Hugo was concerned. 'Caroline, this is my cousin, Claudia.'

As soon as she spoke her cousin's name she knew she shouldn't have. Caroline would go back to Hugo and probably mention... But perhaps not. Caroline was completely unaware of her link with Hugo. She hadn't remembered her from the hotel in the Lake District and she hadn't seen her with Hugo at the opening, so, as far as Caroline was concerned, Angel Weston and her cousin Claudia would mean nothing to Hugo Drake-Latimer—so why mention she had just bumped into them in the bar? But Caroline was Miles's wife's cousin and Hugo was a friend of them both... Her mind went numb.

'Nice to meet you again, Angel,' Angel heard through the dull beating of her heart which filled her ears. 'I expect we'll run into each other again some time.'

Over my dead body, Angel thought numbly, which was probably imminent, judging by the way her heart was paddling limply around her ribcage.

'She's nice,' Claudia acknowledged as Caroline headed eagerly towards the conservatory. 'Lovely dress, and did you see those serious emeralds? Angel, are you ready to order?'

Numbly Angel sank back down into her seat, knowing the opportunity for flight had been lost. If only her legs would get her out of here, but it was impossible. She'd lost the use of everything!

The head waiter was taking Claudia's order.

Angel couldn't think straight. 'The same,' she uttered helplessly. Oh, dear God, perhaps the fates would be on her side and Caroline and Hugo would have left by the time they were ready to be shown to their table. She jumped as the waiter immediately suggested that they follow him through as there was a vacant table at the far end of the conservatory.

The fates *were* on her side, however. Their table was tucked behind a group of foliage that not even Hugo's eagle eye could penetrate. Angel willed herself to relax. Nothing was going to happen. She was over-reacting. Everything was going smoothly.

Claudia sniffed. 'Have you a tissue, Angel?'

'Yes—yes, of course.' She reached down by the side of her chair for her evening bag, where she would have put it if she'd had it with her. 'Damn, I've left my bag in the bar,' she breathed faintly.

It wasn't surprising, she thought as she shakily made her way back to where they had been sitting. She could forget her brains on a night such as this. Fortunately no one had taken up the seats they had just left; in fact the bar was very quiet now, most of the customers having adjourned to the conservatory restaurant. Her evening bag was lying where she had left it. Her panic pulses faded as her hand locked around it. But then her panic pulses lurched fearfully as a hand locked over hers.

'Fancy meeting you here again.'

Her eyes widened with shock as she gazed into Hugo's eyes. He must have seen her crossing the conservatory and left Caroline to come and speak to her. Immediately her senses were on red alert. Caroline must have said she was here, and with her cousin Claudia. Had he seen Claudia too? Had he recognised her as the women he had seduced for money?

'Y-yes, f-fancy,' she stuttered, wondering if she was to have a permanent speech impediment from now on. She couldn't form a proper sentence to save her life.

'And where is Patrick?' he asked smoothly, his eyes darting to the direction she had come from.

Angel felt a huge rush of relief. He wouldn't have asked that if Caroline had mentioned Claudia.

'I . . . I'm not here with Patrick.'

A dark brow rose in surprise. 'Dining alone?'

She shook her head, achingly aware of his hand still clutching her wrist. 'I . . . I told you. I'm . . . I'm not seeing Patrick any more.'

'That's not what I asked you. I asked if you were dining alone.'

Angel glared at him, the thought of him dining with Caroline again giving her strength. 'No, I'm not dining alone.'

'My, you're a fast worker.' His voice was scathing. It infuriated Angel. She wrenched her wrist from him.

'I'm dining with my cousin . . .' She immediately bit her lip. She saw the evening swimming away from her on a rising tide of hopelessness. Hugo and Claudia, herself and Caroline, washed out to sea and drowning in a tangled web of deceptions. 'My cousin Claudia,' she uttered meaningfully. Sink or swim. Angel lifted her chin and gazed at him defiantly. 'Does that name mean anything to you?'

He looked mildly surprised. 'Should it?'

Angel *wasn't* surprised by that. What had she expected—a full confession and a plea for mercy?

'No, of course not. Why should I think it would? Caroline is still flavour of the month, isn't she? Dining with her *again* tonight.' Her voice was all sarcasm in defence of her own feelings. 'My, you do see a lot of each other in romantic settings, considering you're just good friends.'

His smile mocked her evident jealousy. 'For what it's worth, the night was Caroline's suggestion——'

'It isn't worth anything, Hugo, because——'

'For services rendered,' he went on, ignoring her interruption. 'And not the sort of services rendered you obviously think.'

'I don't think where you're concerned any more, Hugo.'

'That's evident, but I'd like to put the record straight, for my benefit more than anything,' he said darkly. 'I don't like having sarcastic insinuations directed at me. I don't bed Caroline and I've no intention of bedding her in the future, and tonight she is wining and dining me in gratitude for financial advice.'

'Huh, and how much have you embezzled from her? The going rate? Or do you assess your victims on their individual monetary status?'

Angel coloured deeply as she spoke, the words, which were spurred by the whole ghastly evening, crowding her senses with misery. She hadn't meant to say it and still she didn't believe him capable of such a thing, but it had just come out, urged by a need to hurt. She regretted it bitterly now because Hugo was gazing at her as if she had just waded out of a slimy pond.

'I . . . I'm sorry,' she uttered weakly. She went to hurry away but he caught her arm. His eyes were furious now, as if her words had taken time to sink in and were now registering loud and clear.

'Not so fast, Angel. What the hell do you mean by that?' he grated angrily.

Angel steeled herself because he had no right to be angry with her. The fury was all hers, against herself for allowing love to overrule her.

'I'm sorry,' she repeated. 'It was a spiteful thing to say and——'

'It was a very odd thing to say, Angel, and a very dangerous thing to say. It implies my integrity is in question——'

Angel's anger flared as his grip on her tightened. 'Well, perhaps it's time your integrity was put under the spotlight,' she seethed. 'Since meeting you I've given you the benefit of the doubt. I refused to believe you capable of such a thing but——'

'What thing?' Hugo grated, his eyes glinting with rage. 'What the hell are you talking about, Angel?'

Angel knew then that she was in too deep. She couldn't handle this; it was way out of her league. A great weariness hit her. She didn't want to be here. Hugo was too much for her, and giving him the benefit of the doubt was too much for her.

'Let go of my arm, Hugo,' she said quietly, the sudden softening of her tone causing him to slacken his grip. She looked into his puzzled dark eyes. 'I'm going back to my table now, to join my cousin. If I thought it would do any good I would insist on your meeting her, but I think that would cause a lot of unnecessary distress to all and I think we've suffered enough.'

He let go of her arm and stared at her. Then he shook his head.

'Angel, I don't know what's going on here but——'

'You don't recognise another brush-off when it stares you in the face?' she retorted. 'Well, you'd better believe this is the final one, Hugo. Leave me alone!'

She turned away, not able to bear the look of puzzlement and disbelief in his eyes. She felt those eyes on the small of her back as she crossed the bar to the conservatory, and it hurt as if it were a knife wound. She was shaking by the time she got back to Claudia, trembling with all that was lost. She sat down and Claudia gazed at her with the same puzzlement Hugo had.

'What on earth's the matter with you?'

How could she explain? What could she say? Suddenly Claudia's attention was drawn away from her and in that fleeting moment Angel experienced true panic as her eyes followed Claudia's. Hugo was urging a confused Caroline to her feet, in full view now as he steered her around the table. His face was a mask of anger, his shoulders tense. Caroline was flustered, gathering up her bag in a hurry as if the hotel were on fire. They skirted another table and headed for an exit and Angel closed her eyes, waiting for some sort of screech of recognition from her cousin.

'Wow, lucky Caroline,' Claudia breathed in envy. 'He's gorgeous.'

In horror Angel blinked open her eyes. She tried to work her mouth and managed eventually to croak, 'D-don't you know him?'

Claudia grinned impishly. 'Much as I love you, Angel, I have to say that if I did you wouldn't be sitting where you are now. He would!'

Angel's mouth dropped open, her stomach somersaulted and her heart leapt.

'You . . . you don't recognise him?'

Claudia, still grinning, widened her eyes. 'I've never seen him before in my life but I'd like to, again and again.'

Angel covered her face with her hands.

'Angel?' Claudia whispered at last, and reached across the table and eased Angel's hands from her face. 'Whatever's wrong?'

The tears were streaming down her face. Tears of relief and happiness and hopelessness. Tears of regret and everything else. People were staring. Even through her tears, Angel was aware that people were staring. She sniffed and smiled through a blur and fumbled in her bag for a tissue.

'Claudia, that . . . that man, that gorgeous man with Caroline, is . . . is the man . . . the man I love. Hugo Drake-Latimer!'

This time it was Claudia's mouth that dropped open.

CHAPTER TEN

ANGEL stared across the causeway, letting the engine idle as she sat in her car wondering if she was doing the right thing and wondering what sort of a reception she would get from Hugo.

For days she'd trawled her memory for the good things that had happened between them, ignoring all the nasty things, and she had convinced herself that he would want to see her again. But so much had happened in the last week, enough to knock his life sideways, enough for him to seek solitude in his secret hideaway.

It was a glorious day, the sun shining brightly in a clear blue sky. The lake ahead was at peace with the world, calm and still, fringed by lush pine forests. Angel could clearly see Greystone Cottage at the end of the causeway—the place where she had fallen in love with a crook and a womaniser, a man she had loved by chance.

Taking a deep cleansing breath, Angel shifted the gear into first and accelerated slowly across the causeway. She prayed that he would hear the car engine and come out to greet her, take her in his arms and understand and make it easy for her.

She felt she was being watched as she crossed the causeway, but maybe it was just her imagination fooling her. She knew it was as she pulled up on the shingle drive outside the cottage. There was no sign of life but she knew he was here because Miles had told her he would be.

The front door was closed but not locked and Angel tentatively pushed it open, glad that she wouldn't have to suffer the indignity of hammering on the door and waiting for him to answer. His study door was ajar and she could see him seated at his word processor. She marvelled at her own courage as she stepped silently into the room and stood behind him. She read the screen and her heart leapt. 'Angel pure, Angel bright, Angel available?'

It was the most beautiful question mark in the world. A hopeful question mark. He must have seen her approaching. Her heart glowed.

'I must have taken a wrong turning somewhere,' she murmured softly behind him. 'I seem to be lost. Perhaps you can help?'

He didn't move, not a muscle. She gazed adoringly at the back of his head, her heart so full of love it was fit to burst. But she couldn't tell him yet because there was so much else to be got through. There was a conscience to be cleared, a mountain of misunderstandings to be sifted through, a plea for understanding from him.

She placed her hands on his shoulders and felt the tension under her fingers. He'd been through so much, and she bit her lip, wanting to ease it all away from him.

The new Angel spoke for her, not the Angel pure of a lifetime ago.

'I want to make love with you,' she said tenderly. 'Not later, now, because that's the way it is sometimes.'

She thought he might be smiling; she hoped he was. Slowly one hand came up and covered hers on his shoulder.

'Do you know what you're saying, Angel?'

She grazed a thumb across his fingers and smiled to herself. 'Yes, I do. There's a certain type of woman that's attracted by the criminal element in a man. I fell in love with a crook and a womaniser and there was nothing I could do about it.'

Slowly he turned and looked up at her. His face was drawn but there was new life in the gleam of his eyes. She knew with a fluttering of her heart that she was the cause.

He smiled. 'So I fell in love with a gangster's moll, did I?'

'I don't know who you fell in love with, Hugo,' she murmured. 'I followed you here that first night after hearing your name mentioned at the hotel. Claudia had told me all about you and fate seemed to have thrown you at me. I followed you, thinking I could get some sort of retribution for my cousin. I ended up falling in love with you and making love with you. Somewhere along the way I lost the real me.'

'You discovered the real you, Angel, and you've put me through a hell I never wish to encounter again, and you're damned lucky I don't put you over my knee and give you a good thrashing.'

Though his words were harsh they were tempered with humour. He gripped her hands and with a mischievous smile she bent and murmured across his lips, 'Oh, please do.'

He pulled her down on to his lap, but he hadn't a good thrashing in mind. His lips were heated with desire on hers and she clung to him, knowing that it was going to be all right, but also knowing that she had a lot of explaining to do.

'Hugo,' she uttered weakly, but he gave her no chance to utter another word. He stood up, scooping her up with him.

'Love first, penance later—that's if you've any strength left to explain the she-devil element in you.'

'You're taking this awfully well, Hugo,' she gasped as he tossed her down on to the bed upstairs.

'Yes, I am rather,' he acknowledged as he lay down beside her and proceeded to unbutton her silk shirt. 'Trouble is I tend to throw caution to the wind when you're around. You came into my life in suspicious circumstances and I was helpless from then on. You have one redeeming factor going for you, though, and it's the one reason you're here, about to be made love to instead of being sent away with a flea in your ear.'

'Oh, and what's that?' she gasped as he ran his fingers over the soft rise of her breast.

'The most beautiful breasts in the world,' he uttered helplessly as his mouth brushed over her sensitive skin.

Angel writhed under him, desire flooding her very being till nothing mattered in the world but to be loved by him.

'I . . . I can't believe my breasts are the only reason you have forgiven me,' she whispered.

He shifted slightly to ease her jeans over her hips and bent to run the tip of his tongue over the soft planes of her stomach.

'Who said anything about forgiveness, Angel?' he breathed against her. 'You've a lifetime of this sort of punishment ahead of you. Who said crime doesn't pay?'

She smiled up at him as he eased away from her to remove his jeans and shirt, and then she held her arms and her heart open to him and he came to her. This unpredictable man who understood so much. This villain of hearts.

They loved slowly at first, soft movements that teased and tantalised. Their kisses were binding, the contact of their flesh a promise of love forevermore, and then when the heat had built up they let themselves go to the frenzied passion of their union. Hugo moved into her deeply and with such command that she let herself go to his power, moving with him and showing the power of her own love as together they rode the crest of sensation till there was no strength left. Their climax was cathartic, heady with feeling and sensuality, and so deeply moving that they couldn't speak for a long time after.

Angel lay on her back with Hugo's arm possessively across her waist. She ran her fingers over the warm skin of his arm, soft, soothing strokes of comfort for all he had been through. It had all been Ralph's fault, she knew that now.

'How long do you think he'll get?' she mused.

Hugo stirred next to her, rolling over on to his back and staring up at the beamed ceiling.

'Ralph Arnott?'

'Who else?'

He laughed. 'I thought you might be referring to me. I reckon I'm in for a life sentence.'

Angel leaned up on one elbow and gazed down at him. She smiled demurely but her eyes were glistening with mischief. 'Is that a marriage proposal?'

He looked deep into her expectant eyes. 'Do you want it to be?'

She laughed lightly. 'It's easy to see why you turned to a life of crime—the written word, of course. Questions, questions. Where's the romance in your life?'

'Coming up, I'd say,' he uttered meaningfully, and took her hand as if to direct it somewhere, but she drew it back with a small screech and sat up.

'You're insatiable!'

'I'm in love,' he pleaded, and pulled her back. He rolled over her to prevent her escaping.

'Do you want to talk?' he asked, and Angel nodded.

'We should have talked before we made love——'

'We should have talked from the off,' Hugo corrected. 'But because I've such insight into what makes people tick I forgive you for all you've thought of me.'

'But you must have been hurt to think I believed all those things about you, Hugo,' Angel insisted.

'You didn't ever believe I had cheated women out of their wealth, Angel, otherwise you would never have let me love you. OK, you wavered a few times, you had your doubts, and when those doubts became too much for you you backed off. I understand that. The evidence against me must have been overwhelming, but you chose to put your own judgement on me and decide about me yourself. *That* was the redeeming factor that swayed my thinking. You could have shopped me from the off but you didn't.'

'Because I loved you, Hugo, and couldn't believe it was true. Oh, God,' Angel moaned, 'you don't know what I've been through.' She lifted her hands and held his face. 'It never occurred to me that you weren't the Hugo Drake-Latimer that cheated Claudia. When I followed you that night I did believe you were a crook and then, when I got to know you and realised you didn't need to do that sort of thing for monetary gain, I just convinced myself that you must have done it for some sort of research for your books, or even for the thrill of doing something devious.'

'I'd have to be a weirdo for that,' he grinned.

'Oh, you are, a very strange man,' she acknowledged lightly.

'So you believed that I'd had an affair with your cousin at least?'

Angel let her hands drop from his face. 'Yes, I did,' she admitted on a deep sigh. 'I went through agonies of guilt and despair over Claudia and Patrick.' Her eyes suddenly filled with tears. 'But I couldn't help myself loving you, Hugo. I shouldn't have let it happen but it just did. Nothing like you had ever happened in my life before. I lived in a secure, predictable world and suddenly you were thrust into my life as if... as if...'

'I was meant to be,' he finished for her. His eyes were soft with loving as he bent to kiss the tears from her cheeks. 'My poor darling, and I accused you of being a whore at heart.'

'I wasn't, Hugo, I wasn't. The first thing I did when I got back from here was call Patrick to finish our relationship. If Patrick had truly meant anything to me I would never have allowed you to love me. I still felt guilty over what I had done with you, though. I . . . I almost felt I *was* some sort of a whore at heart for allowing it to happen.'

'I'm sorry, darling, and I was a bastard for saying it, but I hoped it might jolt you out of whatever was troubling you. I knew something deep-rooted was getting at you but I didn't know what. I thought you still loved Patrick and I was insanely jealous. I couldn't bear the thought of losing you.'

'And I couldn't bear the thought of losing you, but it was all so hopeless. You made such a big thing of seeing me with Patrick at the opening. There was nothing in it—he wanted to be friends, that's all—and you made me so mad with your accusations. Then Caroline kept popping in and out of your life and then Miles . . . Miles warned me——'

'Miles warned you? About what, for heaven's sake?' he asked indignantly.

'I . . . I think he had you in mind for his wife's cousin, Caroline,' Angel told him hesitantly.

'So he warned you off me?'

'Well . . . well, sort of, I suppose but . . . but of course he could have been thinking of me . . . I mean, I was Angel pure, Angel bright.'

Hugo started to laugh. 'Well, he's in for a shock when I marry you, then, isn't he?'

Angel gasped on a smile. 'Is that another of your veiled proposals?'

He kissed her full on the lips. 'It sounded like it to me.'

Angel twisted under him. 'How can you want to marry me after all that's happened? I accused you of embezzlement at the Riverside.'

'Only because you were beside yourself with jealousy over Caroline.'

'You didn't know that at the time, though.'

'No,' he conceded ruefully. 'I thought you'd gone out of your mind. I was so furious with you, I ushered Caroline out as fast as her legs could carry her.'

'I'm glad you did because if you hadn't Claudia would never have seen you and not recognised you.'

'That doesn't sound right to me,' he teased.

Angel laughed. 'You know what I mean. I nearly died with shock when she said she'd never seen you in her life before, and she nearly died with shock when I told her you were the man I loved and you were Hugo Drake-Latimer!'

'Ralph Arnott used my name for three other deceptions while he was working for my company,' Hugo explained quietly. 'My head of staff grew suspicious when he found discrepancies in his expense accounts, and then one of the women he had cheated kept calling and asking for me, saying she was concerned over a deal we had done together. Seeing as I hadn't personally dealt with a client for aeons, it further aroused his suspicions and he called me in. By then Arnott had done a runner. Thanks to Claudia's coming forward with vital information about him, the police were able to nail him and stop him deceiving more.'

Angel sighed deeply, her eyes wide with sadness for what he must have been through. 'I know. Miles told me the whole story. When you broached the subject of Ralph Arnott with him he gave you permission to delve into his files. I was worried about that, you know, afraid Miles would hit the roof when you stormed off with the information. You should have told me the truth and so should Miles.'

'Neither of us knew you knew anything about it. We were both sickened by the whole business.'

'Now that it's over, Hugo, what are you going to do with your investment company?' she asked with concern. 'You can't live like this, torn between two professions.'

'I'm not torn any more. My brother is taking over the investment company and I'm going to carry on writing.' He lifted a strand of her hair and twirled it in his fingers. 'Is that all right with you?'

She gazed up at him happily. 'It's just perfect with me. A perfect life with my perfect man, and you are perfect, Hugo,' she sighed. 'Miles told me about your reimbursing the women for their lost investments.'

'With interest,' he added. 'It's the least I can do, seeing as they were all seduced under my name.'

'Well, I hope they're not too grateful,' Angel teased. 'Claudia is already madly in love with you.'

'But I'm spoken for, darling,' he told her as he gathered her into his arms. 'Well and truly spoken for.'

Angel twined her arms around his neck. 'Don't you think it strange that those other women didn't come forward before?'

He mouthed kisses across her forehead. 'Not really. I know a certain little lady who obstinately believed that her lover was incapable of felony and kept her mouth shut for a very long time.'

'Ah, but that was because she was in love with the *real* Hugo Drake-Latimer.'

'Stand up the *real* Hugo Drake-Latimer,' Hugo jested, and Angel screeched as he thrust himself hard against her.

'You're a damned villain,' she laughed.

'An insatiable one where you're concerned. Come, let me love you again and then we'll draw breath and discuss our future.'

'We have one, do we?'

He sighed. 'Are you pressing for another proposal?'

'I haven't heard *one* yet, let alone another.'

He teased her lips with his. 'OK, Angel pure, Angel bright. Marry me, be my wife and live with me.'

'On one condition,' she teased. 'You give up playing with women's emotions and their money——'

'I'm innocent,' he mocked, running his hands seductively down her thigh. 'All I want is you.'

'And you have me,' she murmured. 'Completely and utterly and purely by chance. I fell in love with you by chance. If I hadn't followed you that night——'

He stopped his heated exploration of her body. 'You know, you've given me an idea for a new book,' he said reflectively. 'How does this sound? Nightfall, swirling mists over the lakes, beautiful heroine follows a handsome stranger to his secluded island home and——'

Angel giggled and pressed her fingers over his lips. 'Forget it, Hugo, it's been done.'

He gently nibbled her fingers, then laughed softly in her hair, and then there was no more laughter as they wrapped their arms and legs around each other and got down to the serious business of loving and living their lives together forevermore.

TASTY FOOD COMPETITION!

How would you like a years supply of Temptation books ABSOLUTELY FREE? Well, you can win them! All you have to do is complete the word puzzle below and send it in to us by 31st October 1995. The first 5 correct entries picked out of the bag after that date will win a years supply of Temptation books (*four books every month - worth over £90*). What could be easier?

```
H O L L A N D A I S E R
E Y E G G O W H A O H A
R S E E C L A I R U C T
B T K K A E T S I F I A
E E T I S M A L C F U T
U R C M T L H E E L Q O
G S I U T F O N O E D U
N H L S O T O N E F M I
I S R S O M A C W A A L
R I A E E T I R J A E L
E F G L L P T O T V R E
M O U S S E E O D O C P
```

CLAM	HOLLANDAISE	OYSTERS	SPICE
COD	JAM	PRAWN	STEAK
CREAM	LEEK	QUICHE	TART
ECLAIR	LEMON	RATATOUILLE	
EGG	MELON	RICE	**PLEASE TURN OVER FOR DETAILS ON HOW TO ENTER**
FISH	MERINGUE	RISOTTO	
GARLIC	MOUSSE	SALT	
HERB	MUSSELS	SOUFFLE	

HOW TO ENTER

All the words listed overleaf, below the word puzzle, are hidden in the grid. You can find them by reading the letters forward, backwards, up or down, or diagonally. When you find a word, circle it or put a line through it, the remaining letters (which you can read from left to right, from the top of the puzzle through to the bottom) will ask a romantic question.

After you have filled in all the words, don't forget to fill in your name and address in the space provided and pop this page in an envelope (you don't need a stamp) and post it today. Hurry – competition ends 31st October 1995.

Temptation Tasty Food Competition,
FREEPOST,
P.O. Box 344,
Croydon,
Surrey. CR9 9EL

Hidden Question _____

_____

Are you a Reader Service Subscriber?   Yes ❑   No ❑

Ms/Mrs/Miss/Mr _____

Address _____

_____

_____ Postcode _____

One application per household.

You may be mailed with other offers from other reputable companies as a result of this application. Please tick box if you would prefer not to receive such offers. ❑